STAR WARS

DARK LEGENDS

STAR WARS

DARK LEGENDS

WRITTEN BY
GEORGE MANN

ILLUSTRATED BY
GRANT GRIFFIN

DISNEY
LUCASFILM
PRESS

LOS ANGELES · NEW YORK

Printed in the United States of America

First Edition, July 2020

1 3 5 7 9 10 8 6 4 2

Library of Congress Control Number on file

FAC-034274-20171

ISBN 978-1-368-05733-2

Visit the official *Star Wars* website at: www.starwars.com.

For Stephen Paul Mann.
You are my father.
–G. M.

I would like to dedicate this book to
my sister, Nicole, and my niece and
nephew, Leah'Claire and Conway.
The Force is strong with them.
–G. G.

CONTENTS

A LONG TIME AGO

IN A GALAXY FAR, FAR

AWAY. . . .

INTRODUCTION

WELCOME, BRAVE READER, TO

this treasury of all things dark and gruesome. Within, great knowledge awaits.

Before you turn the page, however, take a moment to reconsider . . . for here in your hands you hold one of the most perilous tomes the galaxy has ever known.

Contained within its pages are stories that will curdle your very soul—spine-chilling tales of danger and deceit, of dark lords and fiends, of betrayal and corruption. Once read, these stories will escape into the ether, never to be imprisoned again—for their words are like the powers of the Sith themselves, spinning visions in the nooks and crannies of your mind.

In truth, this book is brimming with secrets that should never be told.

Herein, too, lies a despicable certainty: the galaxy is rife with terror. It crowds the shadows, lurks at the threshold, watches from behind every half-closed door. The dark side is ever present, waiting to tempt the unwary, to make monsters of the benign, to twist the bright spark of the imagination toward fear.

Yes, the ways of the dark side are insidious indeed, but they are not unknown—not if you know where to look.

Or should that be . . . where *not* to look?

If it must be so, draw a deep breath, steady your

hand, and prepare yourself for what is to come. And do not dare to claim you were not warned.

One last time, then . . . are you sure you wish to read on?

The Orphanage

 N THE PLANET
Gaaten, nestled amongst the
gloomy spires of a once great
city, sit the ruins of an orphan-
age where, long ago, children who had lost their
parents during the fallout of the Clone Wars were sent
to be cared for while they awaited placement in new
homes throughout the sector.

Only, all was not well at the orphanage, for
amongst the children there were tales of a dark terror
who came in the night: a tall, thin man with sharp
teeth and glowing eyes, who from time to time would

visit the orphanage to steal away children, scooping them out of their beds and dragging them through the window, their cries muffled and unheard. The children who were taken by this horrifying creature were never heard from again.

These rumors were passed in terrified whispers between the children, muttered beneath bedsheets or behind cupped hands when the lights went out. The stories had, of course, been dismissed by the orphanage staff, and while it was true that some children had gone missing from the orphanage over the years—probably nothing more than runaways, children unhappy with their lot and suffering from the devastating loss of their parents—the rumors were viewed as nothing but the wild imaginings of disturbed youths, an embodiment of their fear and pain. Nevertheless, the stories persisted, and there was little the orphanage staff could do to curtail them.

All who came to reside in the orphanage, then, heard tell of this monster and, from that moment on, lived in fear that they, too, might become its next unwitting victim. All except one.

Elish had always been considered an exceptional child, ever since her time at the school on Malloran, where she had astounded her teachers with her confidence and scholarly aptitude. She was a gentle sort, prone to helping others before herself, and that had made her popular with her peers and the younger children alike. Like her mother—a palace guard on Malloran—Elish had always felt a deep connection to the universe around her and all the living things that inhabited it. This connection granted her a great sense of peace, and while she, too, had witnessed horrors, she refused to believe in whatever dark phantom the other children at the orphanage feared. For Elish, evil was embodied not in the form of monsters but of men, for she understood that all the terrors that had so recently blighted the galaxy were enacted at the behest of individuals and not creatures of the night.

So it was that Elish, upon coming to the orphanage on one of the Empire's vast transport ships, became something of a steadying force to the other children, helping them cast aside their fears and, despite all they had lost, seek peace amidst the dormitories and schoolrooms of the ramshackle old building.

For many months this went on, and much to the delight of the orphanage staff, talk of the phantom faltered. The children seemed altogether happier, and when the supply ships came in for the season, some of the orphans were allocated new homes with adoptive parents eager to lavish love and attention on their new charges.

It was not unusual for Elish to be awoken at night by the sound of screaming—for some of the children in the dormitory were plagued by night terrors that would wrench them from their slumber, causing them to lurch up in their beds, their faces gleaming with sweat. Never would the night staff come to comfort the poor children, so Elish would slip from her bed to take their hands, and her calm words and comforting influence would be enough to quiet their nightmares and send them readily back to sleep.

However, one night not long after her arrival, there was a great disturbance during the night, and all around Elish the alarm went up. She leapt from her bed to find the entire dormitory in disarray, and word amongst the children was that the monster had paid a visit in the small hours of the night and stolen away a young boy named Samil.

True enough, there was no sign of Samil, and search as they might, none of the staff or the children could locate him. Nor was there any evidence that a stranger had come amongst them, save for the window gently tapping in its frame, stirred by the breeze because the latch had been left undone.

After securing the window, the orphanage staff soon began ushering the children back to their beds, cooing sympathetically, shushing their cries of distress. Samil would be found in the morning, they said, or else he'd decided to run away and leave them, sneaking off into the night to make his own way in the world. Elish, though, could see that Samil's handful of belongings had been left behind, scattered beneath his bed—and she knew he would never have left his toy heroes behind, for he would never tolerate being separated from the little hand-carved figures.

Thus, as the other children finally began to settle once again in their beds, Elish lay awake, reaching out with her senses, for she had come to recognize Samil through his connection to the universe, similar to her own. This had marked them out as different from the other children—all save perhaps one other, a young Kessurian girl named Gee'far, who also seemed to share Elish's unusual perspective.

Sure enough, though, Elish could sense no trace of Samil anywhere within the confines of the orphanage or its grounds. Discomforted, she lay awake for the rest of the night, certain that he would not be found the following day.

The next morning a small expedition was put together from amongst the staff, which set out for the village, hoping to discover that Samil had fled the short distance to the settlement during the night. They were certain he would be found, cold and embarrassed, huddled in someone's barn, ready to return to the orphanage for a warm bath and a rest.

As Elish had predicted, however, the team returned but a few hours later, tired and hungry, claiming that there was neither word nor trace of the boy in the village, or anywhere on the surrounding paths and roads. He had simply vanished, and there was nothing at all they could do about it.

The next day the rumors of the dark terror returned as the children whispered about the sounds of scratching they had heard at the window, the hissing breath of the creature as it had moved amongst their beds, the icy cold that had signified its arrival. Despite the best attempts of the staff, the children muttered to one another in fear, terrified of what might happen if the dark terror came for them next.

Over the course of the next few weeks, Elish made a point of befriending Gee'far. The Kessurian girl was almost two years younger than Elish, but much like Elish, she carried herself with a surety and confidence that belied her youth. They took long walks together around the grounds, explored the nearby ruins, read stories, told each other tales of the Clone Wars and the dreadful things they'd seen, and studied together under the tutelage of the stern old lady who ran the orphanage school. They swapped bunks to be closer to each other, and each night, as Gee'far drifted off to sleep, Elish would stay awake as long as she could, watching over her friend and watching the dormitory window for any sign of the monster. For, after Samil's shocking disappearance, Elish had begun to wonder if there was truth to be found in the terrible stories of the yellow-eyed phantom, after all.

Time passed, and as it did, life at the orphanage returned to relative normality. Soon the transport ships would arrive with their seasonal supplies, and there would be a new influx of children to the orphanage— as well as a handful who would leave, off to settle in new homes far away on other worlds. The place became a hive of activity as preparations were made.

Elish still thought of poor Samil from time to time, but after so long, she had once again begun to doubt the stories of the phantom. Perhaps Samil really had run away—he hadn't been happy at the orphanage, after all—and had simply hidden from the search parties. Perhaps he was out there somewhere, hiding amongst the ruins of the old city, making a new life for himself on his own terms. Yet Elish was still filled with a gnawing doubt; if he was out there, wouldn't she have sensed his presence, as she did with Gee'far when they were apart during the day?

For many weeks she had maintained her watchful vigil over the younger girl, but wakefulness takes its toll after a time, and Elish was weary, deep down to her bones. So it was that, when Gee'far settled down to sleep one night, Elish felt her own eyes closing, unable to stay awake any longer to watch over her friend. . . .

But from this unintended slumber, Elish suddenly woke with a start. All was silent in the dormitory, save for the quiet murmur of sleeping children all around her. A gentle breeze brushed her cheek and she stretched, rolling over onto her side to peer at the window. The curtain billowed softly in the breeze, shimmering in the moonlight. She started. The window was open!

Elish sat up, sucking air into her lungs. She turned to Gee'far . . . only to find that she was too late.

The crooked, stooped figure of the phantom loomed over her friend's sleeping form. He was dressed entirely in black, with a strange metal disc attached to a panel on his back. His eyes were aglow with the brightest yellow and seemed to weep tears of blood down his stark, pale cheeks. His head was hairless and gray, with strange red markings describing patterns on his pate. His body was tall and thin, his arms gangly and ending in long, slender fingers, and as he stooped lower to gather Gee'far up in his grasp, stifling her protests with a hand held firmly across her mouth, he looked directly at Elish, smiling wickedly to display his jagged, feral teeth.

And then he was gone, moving so swiftly that Elish could barely make sense of what she was seeing. He seemed to flit amongst the shadows, bounding over children's beds in effortless leaps, until he was standing just before the open window, one foot on the ledge. Elish—who had been rooted to the spot, unable to move, to emit even a single sound—fought desperately against the strange force that bound her, pushing back against it with her mind, with her feelings . . . and for a moment she thought it might give, that she might free herself to do something to help her friend.

At this the dark terror paused in the open window

and, framed horribly by the moonlight, looked back at her, inclining his head appreciatively, before stepping out into the frigid night beyond.

Immediately, Elish felt her senses return to her, and she screamed.

The lights went up and the staff came running, but of course, there was nothing to be done. There was no sign of the phantom from the window or amongst the ruins below, and all Elish could do was stare at Gee'far's empty bed and weep.

The staff at the orphanage knew Elish for the sensible child she was and did not dismiss her tale of the yellow-eyed man and his wicked smile. They increased their nighttime patrols through the dormitory and fitted a new lock to the window, but in truth there was little else to be done. Further searches proved fruitless, just as they had when Samil had disappeared. Gee'far was gone, and Elish could no longer sense her presence on Gaaten.

Life at the orphanage continued, but a sullen silence had befallen the children, and without Elish's comforting words and gestures, they grew terrified once again that the evil phantom would return.

Elish knew, however, that if he was to come, then she would surely be his next victim, for the dark terror had sensed the strange connection inside her, felt her push back against his awful, smothering control, and she knew that was what he hungered for. Had not Samil and Gee'far both shared her deep understanding of all that went on around them? Wasn't that why they were taken?

She knew that something had to be done. From that day forth, each morning before the other children rose, Elish would sneak from the dormitory, through the echoing halls of the orphanage, and out into the ruins of a temple close to where she and Gee'far had once played. There, she would scale the jagged remnants of the temple's spire, find a perch for herself close to its apex, and call out through the vast web she could feel thrumming around her, begging for help from any who might hear her plea.

For many days this continued, and Elish grew increasingly despondent, fearing the imminent return of the yellow-eyed phantom. At last, however, her cry for help was answered.

Someone came that day from the stars, landing in the ruins in a brightly colored ship—a dark-skinned woman named Kira Vantala, who carried the hilt of a strange weapon at her belt and spoke with an authority even the orphanage staff seemed cowed by. Dismissing their concerns, she sought out Elish amongst the children and asked her to explain what had occurred the night Gee'far had been taken.

Carefully, Elish related her tale, and as the woman heard it her face creased in concern, for she claimed she understood what the evil thing wanted and from where it had come. She resolved to put a stop to it immediately.

When Elish told the woman about her own fears of being taken—for she understood intrinsically that she could trust her—Kira explained that she, too, was a survivor, just like Elish, and that although it was widely believed that the wars had ended, it was more important than ever to fight for what they believed in and to protect the innocent from harm, no matter how terrifying it might seem.

So it was that each night for more than a week, Kira Vantala lay in wait, and the children slept more soundly than they ever had before, comforted by the presence of their new guardian. All, that was, except Elish, who knew she was to be the dark terror's next target and that she had to find the means within herself to be brave and help Kira defeat the terrible enemy. Perhaps then she could stop the phantom from taking any more children and in some way make up for what had happened that night with Gee'far, when she'd been unable to help her only real friend.

One night soon after, as she prepared herself for bed, Kira whispered in Elish's ear that the phantom was close. She had sensed his presence on Gaaten and knew that he would come that night to the orphanage to attempt another abduction. Elish, too, could feel the creature's nearness, like a tightness in her chest, and she knew that whatever happened that night she would be strong, for only then could the monster be stopped.

Sure enough, as the gloaming finally tipped over to night and the chill dark set in, Elish stirred at a sound from the window.

Slowly she turned, holding her breath, expecting to see the terrible apparition peering through the glass panes . . . but to her horror she discovered he was already looming over her bed, just as he had over Gee'far's.

With that terrifying smile writ large on his face, he stooped low and scooped her out of her bed, bundling her up in his arms. His touch was cold and yet somehow seemed to burn her skin, but as she cried out, she realized that no sound came from her lips. Whatever power he had over her was strong and oppressive, and she found herself unable to move, to speak. She tried to push him away with her mind as she had before, but struggle as she might, he was stronger, and his grip seemed to tighten until it felt as though his cold fingers had wrapped themselves around her heart.

"The Force is strong in you, young one," he whispered as he carried her toward the window, his breath warm against her ear. He did not look back as he stepped over the ledge, seeming to glide along the currents toward the shadowy ruins below.

Kira Vantala had been ready for him, however, and as the dark phantom carried the terrified Elish off into the grounds of the ancient temple, she followed swiftly behind, calling the creature out. For a moment Elish feared he might run, that he'd carry her away in huge, unnatural strides, off into the darkness, where she'd never be found. Instead, though, the phantom, amused, stopped in his tracks and turned to face Kira, a sneer on his malignant face.

As Kira approached, the evil thing dropped Elish to the ground, stepping over her as he stalked forward to face the oncoming woman—who, Elish now saw from her position on the ground, was just as fearsome as the dark terror in her own wonderful way, strong and brave and bold.

"Kira Vantala," the phantom said, his voice a serpentine drawl. "I admit that I'm surprised. Of all those who might have survived the purge . . . I did not imagine a weakling such as you to be among them."

"Then that was your mistake," said Kira, "for the dark side has forever underestimated me."

At that the phantom laughed, lurching forward, grasping for her throat. Kira, though, knew the terror's tricks of old, and as he went for her she raised the hilt of her weapon and ignited a blade so brilliant and bright that the phantom cringed, shrinking back and hissing like a cornered snake, his arms raised to his face in appalled shock. Such was the intensity of the light that it seemed to sear the creature's very soul, and he stumbled in deference, driven back by the blade's power.

Stern-faced, Kira gestured with a wave of her arm and the monster was cast aside, surging through the air to slam into a tumbledown wall, dislodging a shower of dust and debris as he slumped to the ground.

But as Elish watched, the phantom rose from amongst the debris, hunched and crooked and grinning wickedly. He moved swiftly, flitting amidst the shadows like a wraith, almost impossible to see. Kira twisted, her glowing blade raised, seeking him out. She could not keep up, however, and Elish screamed a warning as she saw him dart forward, striking Kira hard in the back. The woman went down, the hilt of her weapon rolling away across the ground, its fizzing blade extinguished. The wicked creature fell upon her, his savage teeth glistening, but Kira was fast, and she rolled, spinning up onto her feet, her arm outstretched, fingers open.

Elish saw that the hilt of the woman's sword lay twitching on the ground, as if desperate to answer its master's call. It was trapped, however, beneath a wooden beam, which had fallen when Kira had tossed the dark terror into the wall.

By then, the phantom had pressed his attack, looming tall and sinister over his prey. Elish could see the desperation on Kira's face, the fear that she, too, had felt in the evil thing's presence. She knew what she had to do. Her heart hammering in her chest, she lurched to her feet and dove for the hilt of Kira's sword, pulling it free from where it was lodged beneath the beam. As soon as it was in her grasp, the smooth metal hilt flew free, leaping from her hand and soaring through the air toward Kira.

Elish could hardly make sense of what happened next. No sooner had Kira's fingers closed around the weapon's hilt than there was a flash of hissing light and the blade swept forth in a wide arc. The phantom hissed in pain, clutching at his chest and dropping to his knees before Kira. With another gesture of her hand, Kira sent the dark terror tumbling backward, crashing through the remains of the temple wall, which seemed to crumble around him, showering him in stone.

Before she knew it, Kira was at Elish's side and helping her to her feet. Her leg was smarting from the fall, but she knew she'd played her part and been strong as Kira had shown her. Together, they had defeated the phantom. Never would he return to plague the children of the orphanage again. Finally, they were safe, their nightmare over. Elish sighed in relief.

However, when the two of them staggered over to examine the dark terror's remains, they found nothing amongst the pooling shadows but a broken fragment of the wheel he had worn on his back. And when they turned away to begin the slow walk back to the orphanage, Elish was certain she could hear his manic laughter drifting away on the breeze.

HERE WAS ONCE AN
ambassador called Slokin, who
was a collector of ancient treasures. So vast was his collection
that he had built a repository just to store it, and so
undiscerning was his eye that he had filled it top to
bottom and had long before lost all sense of what he
did and did not own. He had often considered pur-
chasing a droid to properly catalogue the collection
but just as often dismissed the idea, for the credits he
might spend on a droid would surely be better spent

procuring yet more treasures to further enhance the collection.

So it was that, on a visit to the Outer Rim planet of Batuu, Slokin happened upon a mask in Dok-Ondar's Den of Antiquities and knew he must have it. It was black and slender, and filigreed with the finest gold, resembling, to Slokin's mind, nothing so much as a skull. It was like no mask he had ever seen—unique in all the galaxy—and he adored such rarities above all else in his collection.

As a respected trader in such goods, Dok-Ondar was happy to oblige in this matter—for a suitable price—and yet, despite the risk to his own purse, he issued a dire warning to Slokin regarding the mask. It was a treasure, he claimed, that was not to be taken on lightly, as it was rumored to be cursed and might have grave consequences for the unwary or unworthy who attempted to harness its power.

Upon hearing this, Ambassador Slokin's resolve only hardened, for he was not superstitious, and if there was one thing he coveted above even his treasures it was power and influence over others. If the object had led to the downfall of others—well, then it was surely because they had not been strong enough to wield it. Thus, with a final word of warning, the mask passed from the hands of Dok-Ondar and into those of the ambassador.

For many days following his purchase of the mask, Slokin was forced to carry out his formal duties. Yet all he could think about was the mask and what secrets it might reveal to him when he finally got it home. The anticipation was almost too much to bear.

So it was that, upon finally returning to his lavish abode, Slokin tasked his adviser, Potniss, with dissuading any callers and threw himself into a full and thorough investigation of the mask. Hours passed, and turning the mask over in his hands, Slokin began to wonder whether the warnings of Dok-Ondar had been naught but superstitious ramblings after all, for he could sense nothing of the power with which the object was said to be imbued. And yet, when he finally placed the mask on his face, almost as an afterthought, the object seemed only too keen to reveal its secrets.

Sitting amongst the plush cushions of his living

chamber, peering through the eye holes of the mask, Slokin at first believed himself to have been somehow transported, for what he saw through the mask was a view of the interior of a vast and opulent palace.

Perplexed, he lifted the mask from his face, only to discover to his immense relief that he remained in the safety of his own chambers. In returning the mask to his face, though, he found himself back in that distant palace, observing the events that were unfolding in the sumptuous court. He was, he realized, being granted the perspective of the original owner of the mask, as events from long before replayed and the original mask wearer's life began to unspool before him.

Intrigued, Slokin peered around in wonder. The audience chamber he found himself in was wondrous:

gilded walls of the most florid designs, velvet drapes, and immense stained-glass windows depicting scenes from a mythology with which he was utterly unfamiliar. Courtiers in the finest dress—albeit somewhat old-fashioned by Slokin's modern standards—milled about the place, sipping from fluted glasses. And there, on a raised plinth at the heart of the proceedings, draped on a golden throne, sat a man who must have been a king or an emperor, so fine were his clothes and so grand the crown that rested on his head.

Slokin watched, fascinated, as he—or rather, the man in the mask—approached the foot of the throne, peering up at the king with sly, narrowed eyes.

"Behold," he said, and Slokin found himself mouthing the words as they were spoken, "I have come to strike a bargain with the king."

At this the king looked down on him with amusement. "And what would *you* have to bargain with?"

"Your Highness thinks me bold and finds me amusing. Yet in truth I hold the key to his very downfall, and he would be wise to pay me heed."

"A threat?" said the king, his tone thunderous. He raised an arm to beckon for his guards.

"No threat, Your Majesty," said the mask wearer, stepping up onto the plinth and leaning closer to the king so they might not be overheard. "As I said, a simple bargain. For I will not speak of the secret pact you have made with your enemy . . . if I am suitably rewarded for my loyalty."

At this the king paled. "What do you know of this?"

"Everything there is to be known," replied the

mask wearer. "Everything you should not wish your subjects to know." He bowed gracefully. "Of course, I have taken the appropriate measures to ensure my safety."

The king opened his mouth as if to speak, but no words issued forth.

"I trust there shall be a suitable title, as well as land?" said the mask wearer.

The king fixed the mask wearer with the hardest of stares. "A title and land there shall be, and, too, a curse upon your head for such insolence." But the mask wearer simply laughed and turned away, disregarding the king's words.

Chuckling, Slokin removed the mask from his face. He was unsure precisely what he had witnessed, but he was most entertained, and pleased, too, with his treasure. He placed the mask on a special stand in his repository, and having celebrated with wine and sweet cakes, he turned to his bed.

Yet all night he could not sleep for thinking about the scene he had witnessed. The audacity of the mask wearer was to be heartily admired, and Slokin found himself feeling envious. After witnessing the success of the original mask wearer's ploy, he was struck by an idea. Might he not follow in the footsteps of greatness? Might he not extract a similar fortune through the very same means?

That week, he was due to meet with the ambassador of the planet Hadros, an Outer Rim world rich in ore deposits that had not yet been claimed by the First Order. He'd heard tales regarding that very same ambassador—tales the man would not wish to become public knowledge for fear of losing his position. Here, then, was Slokin's opportunity. If the ploy had worked for the original mask wearer, why should it not also work for him?

So it was that, when the ambassador arrived later that week to great fanfare, Slokin took great care to ensure the man felt comfortable and disarmed— supplying only the best food, drink, and entertainment; lavishing him with compliments; offering him favorable terms on the import of his goods. All seemed to be going well, with trade deals being agreed on and profit for both nations a certainty.

It was then that Slokin struck, cornering the

ambassador in his quarters after dinner and whispering in his ear, blackmailing him in much the same way as the mask's former owner had blackmailed the king.

Disgusted, but unable to deny the rumors, the ambassador reluctantly agreed to Slokin's terms, an' soon after Slokin found himself in possession ' small fortune in minerals and precious metals.

Slokin, delighted, took this to be a ' Dok-Ondar's stories had been right and th indeed, retain some residual power. T' curse, he knew, meant nothing—th just a reference to the old king' certainly not be dissuaded. Ev' mirrored those in the life of '

So that very night, as Potniss and the other servants slept, Slokin crept from his bedchamber to the repository, took the mask from its stand, and placed it once more over his face.

He shivered with relish as the image resolved before his eyes. He was in the suite of a well-to-do person, a middle-aged woman, who—judging by the robes she wore and the chains of office around her neck—appeared to be some kind of politician.

The mask wearer was sitting on a low couch, his s crossed, sipping something pink and tasteless from ass. He watched as the politician paced, agitated, y unhappy with something the mask wearer had as he attempting to blackmail her, too?

annot be done," she said, folding her arms chest. "My position—"

"But consider the possibilities, Madame Secretary," urged the mask wearer, leaning forward and placing his glass on the table beside another, which Slokin presumed to belong to the woman. "Consider the profit."

"But what good are credits if they mean deserting my people? I cannot stand for it. I won't." She crossed to the window, peering out at the traffic lanes that buzzed back and forth before her.

"And that is your final word on the subject?" said the mask wearer.

"It is." She did not turn away from the window as she spoke.

"Very well." The mask wearer leaned forward again, as if to reclaim his drink, but instead produced a tiny bottle from the sleeve of his coat. Deftly, he unscrewed the cap and upended it above her glass, allowing the clear fluid to trickle into her drink. Then, as swiftly as the bottle had appeared, it was gone.

The mask wearer stood, collecting both glasses. He walked over to the window, handing the tainted glass to the woman. "Then that is the end of the matter," he said. "Let us drink to your integrity." He clinked his glass against hers and then downed his drink. She followed suit, the relief evident on her face.

For a moment at least.

Slokin watched, thrilled and scandalized, as the woman clutched suddenly at her throat, her eyes widening with shocked realization. She emitted a wet, gurgling rasp, lurched forward as if to grab at the mask wearer, and then sank to the floor, her body twitching as she died.

The mask wearer dropped to his knees beside the crumpled form of the woman. Carefully, he lifted the chains of office from around her neck, weighing them in his hands. "It is a heavy burden I take on, Madame Secretary, but I shall do it in honor of you."

Silently, Slokin slipped the mask from his face. The mask wearer had progressed in his tactics. This was a bold man indeed! Not only had he blackmailed a king, he had killed to achieve political power and influence. Slokin was breathless with admiration. Here was a man who simply took what he wanted. He allowed no one to stand in his way.

The mask was showing all this to Slokin, using its

power to guide him toward greatness. From that day forth he resolved that he, like the original owner of the mask, would take whatever he wanted, no matter the consequences or the cost.

That night, Slokin went to his bed harboring the darkest of thoughts. It had worked before—the mask had led him toward great riches. Now it had shown him the way to great power, too. He made his plans, and the following morning, he put them into motion.

Thus, with a mix of trepidation, nerves, and glee, Slokin set about obtaining a vial of poison—a clear and deadly substance derived from the Achinios weed from the planet Routh. It took nearly three weeks to arrange, during which time Slokin grew increasingly impatient, but sure enough, Potniss proved a loyal servant and the vial was soon pressed into Slokin's sweaty palm, mere hours before he was due to meet with his superior, Gorson, for a formal review of proposals to build a new spaceship construction yard.

The man's pudgy, genial face was flushed upon Slokin's arrival at his office, so Slokin suggested they take a moment to share a cold drink on the veranda before going over the plans. Gorson was only too pleased to oblige—for he was, in truth, a kindly man who would always see to the comfort of his guests— and sent for his protocol droid to fetch refreshments.

Slokin's heart was hammering in his chest, and for the first time since concocting his plan, he began to wonder at the wisdom of it. Did he truly wish to become a killer? Yet the thought of the cool way the mask wearer had set about his task and the promise of the probable rewards was enough to steady his hand as he took the drinks from the returning droid and, careful to act unseen, tipped the vial of poison into Gorson's glass.

Then, taking the drinks out onto the veranda, he passed the poisoned glass to the other man and stood back to watch as events played out before him.

Sure enough, Gorson's warm smile was soon replaced by a horrible, contorted visage as the poison did its work, causing the man to spasm and convulse as he collapsed on the floor. The old man died peering up at Slokin in shock, clutching at his throat and chest in terror.

Despite the horror of it, all that Slokin could feel

was glee at everything that would follow. He took his leave, telling the droid that Gorson wasn't feeling well and wished to remain undisturbed for a time on the veranda.

The next day Slokin woke to the news of Gorson's unfortunate death—of a heart attack—and found himself summoned by the first minister, who, after offering her heartfelt condolences at the sad loss of his friend, asked if he'd be willing to accept a promotion and take on Gorson's duties. Trying to suppress his smile, Slokin readily agreed.

Thus, Slokin found himself taking on a grand position within the machine of the government. All his ambitions had finally come true, for he had been granted both riches and power over others.

Yet Slokin was greedy, and despite his recent gains, that same night he once again crept to his repository and took out the mask, seeking to wear it once more in the hope of procuring even more riches and power.

Only this time the vision was an altogether different proposition—for in it, he bore witness to the mask wearer's terrible murder at the hands of a former ally. The original mask wearer had grown too rich and too powerful, and in doing so had made himself a target, inspiring jealousy in those around him, allowing others to covet his treasure and influence. Thus, the ally—a scruffy young boy who had once been a footman and had carried out a great number of tasks for the mask wearer, aiding and abetting his crimes—had sneaked into the mask wearer's bedchamber and buried a silver dagger in the man's chest before escaping with the mask, claiming it as his own.

Fearful, Slokin tore the mask from his face and fled to his chambers, panicked that he had seen too much, that in mirroring the success of the original mask wearer's life, he might, too, mirror his fall. Was this, then, the curse? Had it been true all along? He barred the doors and allowed no one to enter his rooms but Potniss, his most trusted adviser. Surely, this way he would be safe from harm?

Such was the power and influence of Slokin now, however, that even Potniss could no longer be trusted, for the man had grown tired of his master's demands and secretly coveted Slokin's collection for himself.

So it was that he came for Slokin with a silver knife when Slokin's back was turned.

Paranoid that something such as this might occur—for whom might he trust now—Slokin was ready, and made to run, but the doors were barred and there was no other means of escape. Potniss had thought of everything, and the treasure *would* be his.

Slokin screamed as his former adviser closed in.

So Slokin's life was forfeit, and Dok-Ondar's warning of a curse was proved true. The mask truly was a danger to any who were unworthy of it—and none who had taken it on had yet been worthy. Potniss was soon captured and tried for his crime, and the mask was returned to Slokin's collection. Soon after, a sale of the estate—for Slokin had no family—saw the

items scattered amongst the stars. As for the mask—
well, it resides once more in Dok-Ondar's emporium,
awaiting the next unwary customer foolish enough
not to heed the proprietor's advice.

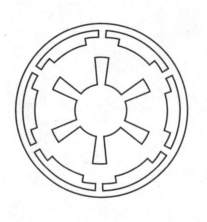

THE
PREDECESSOR

HERE WAS ONCE A great empire so vast and successful that all the many worlds that came to be touched by its influence flourished and sought to join with it, for they understood that to be a part of something bigger was to strive for greatness.

An empire is nothing without its subjects, and each and every one of them, be they engineers or pilots, miners or troopers, had a part to play, like a tiny cog in a great machine, pristine and orderly and working for the greater good.

So it was on the great fleets of starships that sailed across the void, delivering word of the Empire to all the many worlds that had yet to learn of its benevolence. Every individual had a role, and like a well-oiled machine, the ships ran and the people performed their tasks without question or concern.

Questions can, of course, be dangerous things and were not encouraged amongst the crew of such vessels. One day, however, when an Imperial officer named Alger Denholm, who was serving on the Star Destroyer *Exactor*, was called before the ship's captain and promoted with immediate effect, he found himself at something of a loss.

Most Imperial officers in such a position would be brimming with pride at being noticed by ship command in such a way, and while Denholm was sure to offer his most gracious thanks, he was, in truth, perplexed by his sudden and unexpected change in circumstances.

It wasn't that the elevation in rank was unwelcome—merely that Denholm did not understand the reason for the change. There had been no indication that he had gained favor with the captain—indeed, he'd barely spoken to the man prior to that meeting—and even by his own admission, he had done little of note during his recent career that might qualify him for such a sudden alteration in position.

Until the previous day, Denholm had been serving under another officer, Lieutenant Marsden, as he had for some months. It was rare that an officer in the Imperial Navy fraternized with his subordinates or fostered anything akin to a friendship, but Denholm had always found Marsden an honorable man, and as far as he was aware, everything aboard the *Exactor* had been running smoothly and Marsden had been performing more than satisfactorily in his role. Indeed, Marsden was known to have earned a great deal of respect amongst the rest of the crew and was well regarded by Denholm's peers. Additionally, the ship had not been involved in any recent battles or engagements, and there had been no word of Marsden being reassigned to another post or vessel.

Inquiring after Marsden—whose role he had assumed—Lieutenant Denholm was told simply that the other man had moved on and the position had therefore become available. Unnerved—for the whole matter had something of a sinister air about it, particularly in the way the senior officers clearly wished to avoid the subject—Denholm was nevertheless forced to accept his new position without further question.

Still, he could not shake the sense that something untoward had occurred and the matter was being hushed up. Where had Marsden gone? The *Exactor* had been away from port for some time, so the man had not been granted shore leave. He supposed it was possible that Marsden had taken a shuttle, or perhaps even been tasked with undertaking some covert mission off-ship, and Denholm sought comfort in such notions, preferring to think that his former superior had gone on to bigger and better things. After all, was he not on the same career path as Marsden? Might he not someday be charged with a crucial undercover mission, too?

But the lack of understanding nagged at Denholm, for he had always been of an inquisitive nature, and while he understood the need for discretion, his freshly acquired clearance level should have been enough for the other officers to at least offer some indication of what had become of the other man. Denholm was forced to admit to himself that he was nervous, too, for if Marsden had done something to anger the captain, wouldn't it be better for him to know so he could avoid compounding or repeating Marsden's error?

Polite inquiries amongst his new peers also led to telling silence, and soon those peers began to noticeably avoid Denholm, taking the other direction in a corridor, entering and then leaving the officers' mess when they saw he was present. Denholm chose not to challenge them on it, however, believing that the onus was on him, as a newly minted lieutenant, to win them over through his deeds. Perhaps, he decided, they were simply unaware of his skills, his suitability for command. That would be an easy matter to correct.

Thus, Denholm carried on as ordered, stepping up to shoulder his new responsibilities, taking each new task in his stride. Always he strove to present himself in the best possible light to those around him. Indeed, as he settled into his new role, he proved himself more than competent, receiving praise from the captain for the way he'd taken so quickly to the pressures of command. Denholm had given himself wholly to the role, forgoing all else in favor of his duties. No longer did he sit at his desk at night, drawing detailed studies of the flora from the forest moon of Endor for the folio he had been preparing, nor did he join his former friends—now under his command—for meals or the occasional game of sabacc. Instead, he spent his free time taking just that one extra tour of the ship, performing just that one extra inspection of the crew members' uniforms, or studying the etiquette manuals to ensure that his every interaction with the ship's command was beyond reproach.

And yet, in parallel with his rise through the ranks, Denholm found himself growing increasingly isolated as the days passed. Still his peers were uncomfortable in his presence. Still he was shunned by his subordinates—those who had once been his friends. And still he could not help wondering what had become of Lieutenant Marsden.

It was some time into his new role when the first of the bizarre incidents occurred. It was late in the ship's rotation, and Denholm was completing his final rounds when, in the corridor ahead, he caught a glimpse of Marsden. The man was walking as if in a hurry, head bowed. Surprised but elated, Denholm hurried to intercept him, hurtling around a bend, calling his name . . . only to discover, to his embarrassment, that the other man had disappeared before Denholm could reach him. Not only that, but stormtroopers and other officers were staring openly at Denholm, disapproving of his evident lack of decorum.

Confused, Denholm straightened himself out, his cheeks flushing. Forgoing the remainder of his rounds, he headed straight for his quarters. There he poured himself a drink and sipped it shakily, attempting to shrug off his burning sense of embarrassment. Surely it was a simple case of mistaken identity? Another man who looked just like Marsden? If it had been Marsden, he would have stopped at the sound of his name. Yes, that had to be it, Denholm assured himself. Nothing but a misunderstanding.

Still feeling a little uneasy, Denholm retired to his bed, confident that things would have blown over by the morning.

He woke in darkness. The air in his bedchamber was cold, yet he was drenched in a chill sweat that trickled down the back of his neck as he sat up, pulling the sheets tighter around him. Had he heard something? He wasn't entirely sure. It was unusual for him to wake in the night—the thought of all the stormtroopers patrolling the corridors outside his quarters was enough to ensure he usually slept well—but perhaps the strain of the past few weeks was having more of an impact on him than he had thought. He sighed, drew a deep breath, and mopped his brow. He decided it was probably the drink he'd had before bed, churning in his stomach.

Just as he was about to settle down again, however, he heard a sound like someone clearing their throat, coming from the shadows at the foot of his bed.

Startled, he called for the lights, but to his dismay there was no response from the automated systems. He remained in darkness, sitting up in his bed, certain there was someone else in the room. He called out, asking who was there, but the only response was another noise, this time more of a gurgle, like the sound of someone choking and unable to breathe.

Horrified, he lurched to his feet. Whoever was in his room was struggling for breath. He had to get help. He tried the lights again, but still there was no response. He could see the silhouette of the figure, standing at the foot of his bed, clutching their throat. Desperate, he ran for the door and burst out into the corridor, calling for help.

Immediately, several stormtroopers broke from

their patrol to come running, and together they rushed into Denholm's quarters, weapons ready, fearing an attack. But as Denholm stumbled back in behind them, dressed only in the bedsheet in which he'd wrapped himself, he discovered the lights were on, bright and full, and there was no one in the room. Hesitantly, the stormtroopers searched the rest of Denholm's quarters, but there was no sign of an intruder.

Confused, embarrassed, and deflated, Denholm ushered the stormtroopers away, claiming it must have been a bad dream, knowing full well that, as soon as they were out of earshot, they'd be laughing at his expense. The whole ship would probably be laughing at him by morning.

Angry at himself for getting carried away, he flopped onto his bed, but once there, he failed to return to sleep.

The next day, tired from his disturbed night, Denholm nevertheless continued with his duties. He was not so ignorant as to be unaware of the people— mostly subordinates—laughing at him behind his back, but he chose to give them no quarter and remained dignified throughout. Indeed, if anything, he was a little easier on the crew that day than he had been in recent weeks, as if to show that he had nothing to hide and nothing to prove.

Yet, on several occasions throughout the day, he had the most disturbing sense that he was being watched. He could feel a pair of eyes on him, cold and calculating, tracking his every move as he strolled down passageways, sat in conferences, and issued orders to his subordinates. On such occasions he would shudder from the onset of a sudden chill, would feel his heart race and sweat prickle his brow. He knew, instinctively, that he was not alone, that some malign presence stalked him through the ship. He would glance behind him from time to time, turning quickly on the spot, and while this inspired a number of strange or concerned looks from those passing by in the corridors, he could not catch sight of the perpetrator. It was, he presumed, an agent of his peers, set to keep a watchful eye on him and report back with any fodder for their gossiping, but it left him feeling isolated and disturbed.

So it continued, and during the course of the next few days, Denholm felt the presence almost hourly. He became accustomed to it, modifying his behavior, even when alone, trying to ensure he wasn't caught out in some way that could be used to embarrass him before the captain. He tried to catch *them* out, doubling back on his route around the ship, veering unexpectedly in the corridors and ducking through doorways into storage lockers or unused quarters. But no matter what he did, he could not set eyes on the person following him.

His sleep, too, was increasingly disturbed by what he took to be night terrors—during which he would catch glimpses of a pale, twisted face in the gloom and awaken to the sound of choking.

It wasn't long before Denholm's problems came to the attention of the captain, for it was during one of the captain's briefings that Denholm next caught a glimpse of Lieutenant Marsden, walking past the briefing room, his head bowed, his hands cupped behind his back. As Denholm watched, eyes widening, Marsden turned to glance at him through the window, glassy eyes flashing with recognition. Denholm—who had grown increasingly disheveled from lack of sleep—jumped immediately to his feet, crossed to the door, and passed into the corridor midway through the captain's speech. All looked on in horror as Denholm, frustrated, ran up and down the corridor in frantic pursuit of a man they all knew to be gone.

So it was that Denholm was taken to one side by an uncharacteristically concerned captain and told to report to the medical droid for evaluation. Appalled, but only too willing to adhere to the captain's wishes, Denholm did as he was ordered. The medical droid could find nothing wrong with Denholm, however, besides severe fatigue, and issued him a sedative, followed by two days of complete rest.

For the first time in weeks Denholm slept soundly, administered to by the droid, and was back on his feet within the allotted time. He felt refreshed and ready to attend to his duties with renewed vigor, wishing only to put all thoughts of Marsden behind him.

However, a couple of hours into his shift he once again caught sight of the man, hurrying away down the corridor ahead of him. This time, Denholm fought the urge to give chase. It was, he reasoned, the after-effects of the sedatives, or else he was still suffering from exhaustion and needed further rest. He shook off his discomfort and continued with his day, planning for an early night, trying desperately to pretend that everything was going to be all right.

The next day brought further, similar sightings, but Denholm ignored them as before, trying to keep his mind on track. Nevertheless, his behavior became increasingly erratic over the following days as he found himself distracted midsentence by these unwanted sightings, speaking out at Marsden's assumed presence, or lurching strangely at the sound of someone coughing close by. He once again became paranoid that someone was following him and, in fact, that his mysterious stalker was Marsden himself. Perhaps his former superior was trying to tell him something, to speak to him in private or warn him about the eerie choking figure, but for some reason was unable to show himself when others were around. Had Marsden been so disgraced that he could not even show his face? Thus, Denholm took to lurking by himself in the quiet places of the ship, hoping for a clandestine encounter with the man, but no such meeting was forthcoming, and while he felt that cool, lurking presence, he found that he could only catch sight of Marsden at the most inopportune times.

Everyone on the ship gave Denholm a wide berth, and after he attempted to confide in one of his former friends, speaking about the strange things he had seen, even his subordinates began to avoid him whenever possible.

The small, dark hours of the night were increasingly plagued by visitations from the mysterious choking figure, too, and Denholm had taken to staying awake all night to try to avoid the eerie visitor. He grew so tired, however, that he would eventually drift off, only to be awoken by that terrible sound from the foot of his bed, to glimpse the form of the pale figure as it clutched its own throat in terror.

Denholm feared he was going mad—that the stress of the new job and the uncertainty of what had happened to Marsden were leading him to hallucinate. And yet he had no one to talk to. He knew that his work had begun to suffer as, fraught and scared, he was unable to adequately attend his duties. Yet he had to go through the motions, lest he find himself disciplined or court-martialed. His job was the only stable thing left in his life, and he convinced himself that if he could hang on to that, he might yet reclaim his sanity.

So it was that he found himself—despite another sleepless night, during which the strange apparition had been most persistent in its harrowing appearances—wearing his dress uniform in the main hangar of the ship, along with a dozen brightly polished stormtroopers, awaiting the arrival of a visiting dignitary. All Denholm wished to do was get the pleasantries over with as quickly as possible and hand the visitor off to a colleague. He felt nauseated and edgy, constantly peering out of the corner of his eye in case he saw Marsden wandering the hangar or sensed the man's familiar presence close by, watching him.

He scanned the serried ranks of stormtroopers, their faces hidden by impassive masks. What were they thinking? Did they know about the person who was following him? Did everyone on the ship know? Did they know, too, what had happened to Marsden? Perhaps, he thought, he should ask—put them on the spot, interrogate them about how much they knew. His hand trembled. He started to take a step forward—and then the sound of an approaching shuttle caused him to flinch and fall back in line.

The ship sailed in gently through the shimmering

port, coming about before easing itself onto the shining floor with a long sigh. Denholm straightened up, clasping his hands behind his back. This would all be over soon. The visiting dignitary was probably some scrawny old ambassador who needed fawning over by the captain. It would be a simple matter to escort them through the ship to their temporary quarters.

The shuttle door opened with a pneumatic hiss, the ramp extending until it rested easily on the floor. At the top of the ramp, framed by the hatchway, was a silhouette in black—tall and imposing. Denholm stiffened. Suddenly, the air around him was cold. He shuddered. Chill sweat beaded on his forehead.

The man started down the disembarkation ramp, boots thundering with every step. His black cloak trailed in his wake. His labored breath hissed through his imperious black mask. Lord Vader, in all his terrible glory.

Behind Denholm, someone made a choking sound. He felt the hairs on the nape of his neck prickle as cold fingers seemed to brush against his flesh.

Denholm screamed. A shrill, piercing cry that echoed throughout the silence of the hangar. He twisted on the spot, eyes bulging at the horrifying sight of a spectral Marsden, clutching his throat as if in terrible pain, lips mouthing something in terror and desperation. His horrible, choking cough was all Denholm could hear, filling his ears, his mind, drowning out all other thoughts.

That was what had become of Marsden. That was

what had manifested in his room each night, what he'd seen in the corridors of the ship, haunting his every move, following him from pillar to post—the ghost of his former supervisor.

Denholm lurched back, stumbling, trembling. He collided with a stormtrooper, but he didn't care. The only thing he could think about was getting as far away as possible from that dreadful, nightmarish vision before him.

A hand grabbed his shoulder, squeezing so tight that he whimpered. He felt himself twisted around, propelled by that searing grip . . . to discover it was not a stormtrooper he had collided with, but Lord Vader himself.

The dark lord peered down at him through the

glassy eyes of his mask, and Denholm saw himself reflected in their gleam, tears streaming from his eyes, body racked by terrified sobs. He stuttered something unintelligible, jabbing his finger in the direction of the specter. But Lord Vader did not reply.

Denholm, appalled, tried to make sense of what was happening. But it was only as he felt the vicelike grip of spectral fingers close around his own throat that he realized the ghost of Marsden had been trying to warn him. He'd followed Marsden's path all too closely. The fate that had befallen his superior was soon to be his, too.

His body jerked as he was lifted from the ground. His fingers went to his throat, clawing at the terrible invisible hands that were crushing his windpipe. The choking sound filled his ears again, only this time, he knew it stuttered from his own breathless lips.

Denholm's last sight before he crumpled to the ground was his own reflection in that terrible, haunting mask, his last sound the satisfied rasp of Lord Vader's laboring lungs.

The very next day, a young officer by the name of Saul Toten was summoned to the captain's office, where he found himself inexplicably promoted with immediate effect.

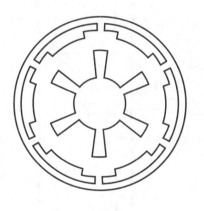

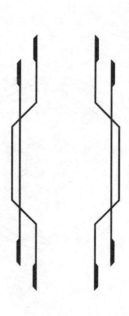

BLOOD
MOON

IN THE FARTHEST REACHES
of the unexplored regions of Wild Space,
the moon of Lupal circles a dying star
whose heart is formed from a core of
the purest kyber. The star is ancient, and the pressures of untold eons have caused the kyber to fracture,
resulting in vast solar flares that erupt from its center—
flickering, angry gouts of red, as if the damaged kyber
itself is bleeding into the frigid depths of space.

Indeed, in the cantinas of the Outer Rim, it is
claimed that if one sails close enough to the flares, it is

possible to hear the star screaming, crying out in the slow, final throes of its oncoming death.

Such is the fate of Lupal, which, when the heart of the star finally shatters entirely, will be bathed in the burning ejecta of the exploding star and scoured bare, all signs that life ever existed on its surface incinerated by the flames.

Of course, Lupal was not always a world on the verge of oblivion. During the age of the Old Republic, before the fracturing of the star and the advent of the solar flares, Lupal was a paradise of unparalleled reputation. Over many thousands of years, a great civilization had risen and flourished on the moon, a highly evolved culture that revered art and aesthetics, philosophy and tolerance. On Lupal, the native peoples established themselves as one of the great civilizations of their age, but so content were they, so peaceful and inward-looking, that they had never felt the need to take to the stars or establish colonies on other worlds. Thus, when the heart of the star broke—some believe after witnessing the devastation wrought by the wars that had riven the galaxy—the people of Lupal were unprepared for the horrors that followed.

Those early, terrible eruptions from the injured sun were enough to bring their civilization to its knees, bathing the moon in harsh crimson light that heralded oncoming waves of destruction. Those few who were not killed outright by the atmospheric disruption and ensuing radiation managed to flee on evacuation barges sent by neighboring worlds, but the survivors were few and far between and were soon scattered amongst the stars, their once great culture reduced to nothing but memories and ash.

Now Lupal is a ruin, overgrown and littered with the detritus of the great cities that once covered its globe. It is inhospitable and deserted, long ago abandoned to its fate.

Nevertheless, the draw of its former glory has been enough to tempt numerous explorers to seek fortune there over the years, from treasure hunters to historians, thrill seekers to archaeologists.

So it was that one group of explorers, intent on uncovering the secrets of those long-lost people—and recovering, too, what remained of their treasures—set out on such an expedition to Lupal, ignoring all warnings of peril and seeking only glory, knowledge, and wealth.

At first it appeared that fate was on their side, for the expedition leader—a human woman named Fionn Tucat—had planned most precisely, charting the ebb and flow of the solar flares to find a suitable window to make their approach to Lupal.

Thus, the expedition led by Tucat and her associate Romina Foss—along with a hired crew comprising a one-eyed Lasat known as Borzul; a Togruta named Cavrolo Sys; a Shistavanen called Kordus Vrak; and two excavation droids, HCT-10 and RF-U5—landed on a plain on the outskirts of the ruined city of Thrass and hastily established camp.

The day's undertakings went well, and soon the

droids had made a reconnaissance of the area, mapping the surrounding ruins. The radiation emitted by the damaged sun meant that much of the crew's equipment was inoperative; long- and short-range scanners provided unreliable readings, and comlinks returned only buzzing static. Nevertheless, the mood amongst the crew was jubilant, for the riches they had dreamed of for so long finally seemed within their reach. Surely there, amongst the ruins of the fabled city, they would find the treasures they sought.

That night, however, Tucat's predictions of the ebb and flow of the solar flares proved unsound, and the flares began again in earnest, lighting the entire sky red and casting the surface of the moon in a dark, sinister hue. It was an ill omen, for Foss had heard tales of the crimson flares and knew they were said to twist people's minds and infest their dreams with horrors. Many of the expeditions that had preceded them on Lupal had ended in disaster, and more often than not, such failures were attributed to the strange influence of the red light. Tucat and the others had heard those tales, too, but had long before dismissed them as fearmongering, believing them to be the sort of stories passed around by explorers such as themselves to dissuade others who might consider plundering Lupal for the abandoned treasures they wished to protect for their own gain.

As the evening wore on, however, it soon became clear that the flares had brought with them more than mere eerie light—for something about the strange, flickering glow did, indeed, seem to affect the mood of all those present.

It began as little more than a mounting sense of agitation amongst the team, a feeling of annoyance with their fellow crew members. They each began to question the motives of their shipmates and to doubt one another's work, muttering under their breaths or making barbed comments behind one another's backs. At first it was easy to put such things down to sheer exhaustion, for the journey had been long and arduous, and they had spent a great deal of time in one another's company already. Yet they soon came to recognize that something greater was afoot.

None felt this more keenly than the Shistavanen, Vrak, for, despite his wolflike appearance, he was the gentlest and calmest of them all, and the least likely to allow dark emotions to manifest. Yet the red light had stirred something deep and primal within him, and as he paced the perimeter of the camp he was forced to fight feral urges, for he knew he could not allow such terrible instincts to surface.

Alas, as the team settled in to eat that night, huddled around a fire pit they'd dug out on the plain, what might have been a minor disagreement between Borzul and Vrak over who should take first watch instead erupted into a blazing row. Before the others were able to intercede, Vrak had grievously insulted the Lasat, shoving him backward over a fallen pillar and inciting a roar of anger from Borzul that might have been heard for several kilometers in every direction, had there been anyone else on the abandoned moon to hear it. It was all Sys and Tucat could do to separate the warring friends, for the rage of the strange light was upon them both, driving them toward violence.

Soon after, the Lasat retreated to his bed to avoid further confrontation, and all agreed that a good night's rest was needed—that the strain of the expedition and the unexpected return of the solar flares was resting heavy on all their hearts. They agreed that all would be well by morning and their exploration of the ruins could begin in earnest. Ashamed and concerned at how readily he had struck out at Borzul, Vrak agreed to take first watch, after all, and continued to circle the camp as the others slept, focused all the while on keeping his wilder impulses in check.

The next morning, however, all was far from well, as there were signs at the edge of camp that a struggle had taken place. The grass had been churned, showing evidence of frantic movement, and there were rust-colored stains on the ground that might have been blood. Borzul's blaster was lying discarded beside a cluster of small rocks.

Despite a hurried search of the area, Borzul was nowhere to be seen. Suspicion immediately fell on Vrak, but the Shistavanen was found in his bunk, having handed over the watch to Sys during the night as agreed. He had no knowledge of the Lasat's disappearance, and it was eventually decided that Borzul must have risen early and wandered off into the ruins to explore or hunt, perhaps suffering from the effects of the solar flares and wishing to be alone.

They agreed to seek him out, just to be certain, but the scanners were still inoperable and the ruins too dense and overgrown to mount an effective search. Even the droids could find no evidence of the Lasat's trail. He had simply disappeared, and the only sign he had left behind was a torn patch of grass on the very edge of camp.

The mood amongst the remaining crew was sullen and suspicious, and soon a heated debate had arisen as they argued over what to do. Tucat and Foss advocated widening their search, but Vrak was pensive, for he feared he had driven the Lasat away with his anger the previous evening. Confiding in Sys, he explained that his anger had seemed so intense, so primal, that he feared losing control, and if the solar flares continued as they had, the crew should consider restraining him to avoid further confrontation.

Tucat and the others knew of the Shistavanen's gentle nature, however, and understood he felt a sense of responsibility for what had occurred the previous evening. Believing him to be overreacting and hoping that Borzul would soon return of his own volition, they decided to set about their excavations. The increase in solar activity meant that it would be unsafe to evacuate the moon for at least a few days, so it was decided that the mission would continue. Nevertheless, they agreed to keep one another in check and to work on individual tasks to avoid rising tensions, only coming together to compare finds and share meals. That way, they reasoned, they would minimize any friction that might arise between them.

Yet, come evening, Borzul had still not returned to camp, and Tucat had begun to grow worried. If the Lasat had wandered off into the ruins of Thrass, had he found himself trapped or in danger? Or perhaps worse, was there another, less scrupulous expedition working somewhere nearby that had abducted Borzul during the previous night? Perhaps even an unknown creature native to the moon that had taken the Lasat as food?

Further searching was out of the question, however, for the crimson flares were coming with increasing regularity, and the ruins of Thrass, along with the expedition camp, were bathed in red light as dark as spilled blood.

It was in this red glow that Vrak once again began to pace the perimeter of the camp. With every surge from the damaged sun he felt his hackles prickle, his primal instincts threatening to overwhelm him. Try as he might to deny them, he could not, and soon his senses were filled with the scent of fresh blood and warm flesh, and the small part of his mind that still maintained some level of civilization wished that his friends had listened and restrained him, for he knew beyond doubt that this was a battle he would surely lose.

Indeed, as the flares grew in intensity, so did his

urges until, unable to hold back any longer, he threw back his head and issued a terrifying howl, his eyes glistening red and feral in the eerie light. Nothing but beast, guided by the primal urges unleashed by the sun, the thing that had been Vrak fell upon the camp in a blind rage.

The first to go was the droid HCT-10, whose industrial-strength servos proved no match for Vrak's brute strength. The wild Shistavanen wrenched the droid's arms from its sockets, pounding the dome of its head until it split, and HCT-10 went down in a shower of sparks and slurred commands.

Next was Sys, who looked on the Shistavanen in wide-eyed terror as Vrak burst into his bunk. He realized that he should have trusted his friend's instincts and bound him. It was with intense sadness that Sys succumbed to the beast, and it was over in a matter of moments.

Alerted by the sound of the beast's rampage, Foss had risen from her bunk, retrieving the blaster she had hidden nearby earlier that night. She sneaked from her tent, peering out into the red light in search of whatever monster was laying siege to the camp.

At first, spotting Vrak, she felt a wave of relief, thinking that he, too, was on a defensive prowl—but upon hearing her ragged sigh he turned to regard her, his eyes glowing bright red. Blood dripped from his fur, and she understood with horror that he was the one she sought—the terrible monster loose in their midst.

With a growl, Vrak lurched toward her, teeth bared, talons flashing.

Foss cried out, squeezing the trigger of her blaster. The shot struck Vrak in the shoulder, sending him spinning to the ground with a whimper, smoke curling from the searing wound.

Foss turned and ran, calling for Tucat to do the same, and made for the nearby ruins, where she hoped she might take shelter to either wait out the effects of the flares or protect herself from further attack by the enraged Shistavanen.

As she ran, Foss heard Tucat break for cover, too, along with the other droid, RF-U5, and she gave thanks that her alarm had been heeded.

Scrambling over the tumbledown wall that marked

the boundary of Thrass, Foss found herself amongst the ruins of the once great city. Even then, washed in the crimson glow, they retained much of their former glory, despite the slumped buildings and collapsed roofs, the blocked alleyways and sagging roads. She hurried down one such street, leaping to avoid the heaps of crumbling stone, ducking beneath fallen lintels, and weaving through deserted buildings that had once housed families.

Behind her, all the while, she could hear the sound of Vrak sniffing her out, continuing his hunt despite his wounded shoulder, driven insane by the light of the red sun.

The night grew long, and for a while Foss rested, her back against the wall of an old store, her blaster clasped in her hand. Her breathing came hard and fast, her heart thrumming in her chest. She knew she should feel scared, but all she really felt was an intense *anger* at what had happened. This, she knew, was the effect of the red light, even then, permeating her every thought, coloring her view. Would she, too, succumb to its curse if she stayed there long enough? She understood why the moon remained unplundered, why the previous attempts to explore the ruined cities had all failed. The red light was a form of poison, a malign influence that turned friend against friend, ally against ally. It was the essence of corruption, making her doubt everything and trust no one.

This, though, was a battle she was determined to

win. She would not allow the anger to take root and grow. She would fight it every step of the way. And she would make it off that moon alive.

A chilling howl erupted from the ruins close by. Foss tightened her grip on her blaster. Something moved to her left. She shifted, pushing herself away from the wall, twisting her blaster to face it . . . only to discover it was Tucat and RF-U5, emerging from the mouth of a nearby alleyway. She lowered her blaster in relief, waving Tucat over. The other woman looked tired and close to the end of her tether. She was unarmed and walked with a limp, suggesting she'd either twisted her ankle during her escape through the ruins or Vrak had at some point caught up with her.

Foss took a step toward her, grateful that the two of them might escape together.

It was then that the thing that had once been Vrak burst from the upper story of a nearby building, silhouetted against the stark red light, a raving, frothing beast intent only on the hunt.

Foss screamed as Vrak fell upon Tucat, who, resolute to the last, raised her fists in defense, attempting to keep the creature at bay. Foss tried to get a clear shot, but it was no use; the alleyway was too narrow, and she risked hitting Tucat if her shot went wide.

With dismay, she watched as the creature closed in on Tucat, talons gleaming in the moonlight, and as tears pricked Foss's eyes, she heard Tucat call out to her to run.

Blinded by her sheer instinct to survive, Foss ran. Through the shattered city she tore, ignoring the snagging of her clothes, the grazing of her limbs. Behind her, the droid rode a spear of rocket fuel, burning the last of its reserves as it tried desperately to keep up with Foss and to keep ahead of the Shistavanen, who followed at a frenetic pace, howling for more blood.

Foss knew that her only hope of survival was to reach the ship, to risk navigating the solar flares and flee the system, for so long as she remained on the moon she was at risk, not only from Vrak but from the sun's dreadful influence on her own mind.

In the distance the ship loomed large, a glimmering beacon on a stretch of plain. She could hear Vrak closing in on her, and she pushed harder, driving herself forward, step after step. RF-U5 had surged ahead of her, guessing her intent, and had opened the door at the rear of the ship, powering up the systems for takeoff. A few more steps and she would make it.

Foss sensed the monster at her heels, felt the tips of his talons scratch at her clothes . . . and then a roar from out of the darkness caused her to lurch sideways just as Borzul slammed into the running form of the Shistavanen, sending them both crashing to the ground. They rolled, thudding over the rocky terrain, gnashing and snarling as they thrashed at each other—Borzul trying to pin the Shistavanen down, Vrak intent only on finishing off the Lasat who had escaped him once before.

Stunned, Foss lost her footing, going down, her elbow striking the ground and causing her to cry out in pain. She scrabbled, backing away from the frantic battle taking place before her and edging toward the ship. She could feel the backwash of its engines as RF-U5 fired up the controls. The open hatch was no more than a few meters away.

She heard Borzul moan and turned in time to see Vrak sinking his fangs into the Lasat's forearm, grinding his jaw in a motion that caused Borzul to almost falter. She met his gaze and saw the determination in his eyes as he raised his other hand, pointing her to the ship. He was buying her time. She dragged herself up, hobbling as she forced herself to run the last few steps toward the lowered ramp. With a cry of effort, she hauled herself up into the hold, her breath ragged, and ran for the cockpit, dropping into the pilot's chair with a wince.

Beside her, RF-U5 was chattering nervously, urging her to take off. She grabbed for the controls and the ship shifted, rising steadily from the surface.

On the plain below, the Lasat and the Shistavanen fought on, sending up clouds of dust in their wake. Blood spattered the parched ground, and for a moment Foss thought that Vrak had gained the better of the Lasat, but Borzul proved stronger, and with a final roar he sent the Shistavanen reeling. Scrabbling to his feet he turned and ran, and ignoring RF-U5's stream of urgent bleeping, Foss banked the ship, sweeping low across the plain. Running hard, Borzul leapt, grabbing at the ramp and dragging himself up into the ship just as Foss gunned the engines and sent them spiraling into the atmosphere.

As the ship pulled away, Foss's last view of the fateful moon was the sight of Vrak, alone on the plain, raging at the sky, his long, low howl audible even over the burr of the ship's engines.

Together, Borzul, Foss, and RF-U5, the only survivors of their accursed mission, made good their escape, stealing away into orbit and leaving the fateful moon far behind them as they circled the bloated, dying sun. As they settled into the cockpit of the ship, however, the sense of relief palpable amongst them, the red glare of another solar flare shone bright through the viewscreen, causing Foss to raise her hands to her face to block out the strange red light.

Borzul turned to Foss, clutching the bleeding wound on his arm. His eye was a fearful shade of red, his lips drawn back in a terrible, feral snarl.

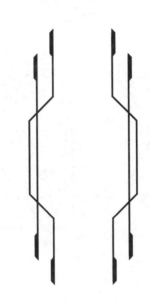

THE **D**ARK
MIRROR

THERE WAS ONCE A Jedi Padawan called Sol Mogra, whose master, Nil Idyth, was such a paragon of virtue that he was known throughout the Jedi Order as the most upstanding Jedi Knight of his time.

Master Idyth's reputation was entirely unblemished; never had he put a foot wrong throughout his long and illustrious career. From his first days as a Padawan in the Jedi Temple on Coruscant to his later years as a Master in the field, he had given only the very best account of himself, and all in the Order looked to him for guidance.

Indeed, Idyth's exploits were often the talk of the younglings, who spun wild tales of his greatest deeds, such as his single-handed liberation of the ice moon of Basath, his defeat of the Swamp Wraith of Phandas, and his banishment of the murderous specter who had once stalked the lower levels of Coruscant. Those were but a few of the triumphs attributed to Idyth, although in truth most went unrecorded, for he had never sought glory, preferring to share his most daring victories with none but the Jedi Council. Nevertheless, despite his modesty, Idyth was recognized as a great hero amongst his peers, and his reputation was unrivaled.

When the young Sol Mogra was chosen as Idyth's Padawan, his heart swelled with pride, for he knew that he was assured the very best training the Order could provide. Simply to be associated with such a virtuous master would earn him respect amongst his fellow Padawans and the younglings.

Sure enough, Sol Mogra's training proved intense but deeply rewarding. Master Idyth did not shy from exposing his Padawan to all the terrors of the galaxy, encouraging Sol Mogra to accompany him on dangerous missions for the Jedi Council, to face monsters both literal and metaphorical. For Idyth believed that to truly conquer one's fear, one must hold a dark mirror to one's heart, to recognize the dangers of a life ill lived, to flinch away from the paths that should never be taken and the choices that should never be made. Only by knowing the path to the dark side might one know how best to avoid it. So it was that Sol Mogra learned the ways of the Jedi and became just as virtuous as his master.

As the years passed, Sol Mogra absorbed all these lessons and more, striving only to make his master proud and to prove Idyth's faith in him well founded. The Jedi Council praised the boy and watched with satisfaction as he slowly shed his childish ways and burgeoned into a worthy young man. Indeed, Sol Mogra soon proved himself ready to be sent on missions of his own, and Idyth was proud each and every time he returned successful, and there to support him each and every time he did not.

It was upon his return from a mission that Sol Mogra first heard the rumors of his master's death. Distraught, filled with anguish and disbelief, he hurried through the Temple—hoping beyond hope that the rumors would prove unfounded.

Yet it was not to be, and upon reaching the council chamber—still encrusted with swamp mud and carrying a brutal wound to his left thigh—he was informed that his master had indeed fallen in battle. Worse, the other combatant had been an assassin, sent—the Jedi Council believed—by a crime boss who wanted Idyth's lightsaber as a trophy for his wall.

Sol Mogra dropped to his knees, struck by a deep sense of loss and appalled by the sudden realization that Idyth had not, after all, been immortal—that, as a

Padawan, Sol Mogra had not cherished every moment as he should, believing his master would forever be there to support him. If the best of them could fall, what did that mean for those such as Sol Mogra, who were still learning to become true Jedi Knights? How could they protect themselves in a universe without Idyth?

All in the Order mourned Master Idyth's passing and shared stories of his valor in remembrance. Yet all was not peaceful in the Temple, for Sol Mogra, riven by grief, petitioned the Council to allow him to seek out the assassin who had felled his master and reclaim Idyth's missing lightsaber. The Council, though, knew that such a mission for Sol Mogra was a fool's errand, for not only would he face terrible danger from a foe even Idyth had been unable to defeat, but in giving in to his emotions in such a way, he would be straying from the path of virtue Idyth had so carefully sent him down. Thus, a team was dispatched not to seek vengeance but to issue a stern warning to the crime boss behind the attack and to reclaim Master Idyth's missing belongings, and all the while Sol Mogra was left to meditate in the Temple, encouraged to seek peace in the Force.

Jedi are not given to sentiment, but there was one item that Idyth had always carried on his person: a wooden amulet worn on a cord around his neck—a relic, he claimed, passed on to him by his own late master. Sol Mogra had long admired the object, for it had the form of an eye, with an iris of glowing kyber embedded deep in the dark engraved wood. Idyth had never been without it—during training, on missions—and believed it to be a totem from an ancient, extinct species who'd once inhabited the galaxy, back before the dawn of time.

In the event of his death, Idyth had made provisions for the amulet to be passed on to his Padawan. So it was that Sol Mogra came to wear the favored relic, after a team recovered the items once belonging to Idyth from the planet Ixilix.

The amulet proved a great reminder of his master's teachings, and by wearing it, Sol Mogra found some measure of comfort, for with the cord around his neck he no longer felt alone. It was as if his master remained with him, by his side at all times, lending him strength and encouragement.

Soon after, despite the grievous loss, circumstances began to improve for Sol Mogra. His missions for the Jedi Council all proved startlingly successful, and he was praised often for his demeanor and the way he comported himself. All at the Temple said he had taken well to his master's training, that he was a most virtuous Jedi in the mold of the late, lamented Idyth.

So it went on for years. Sol Mogra's star rose swiftly within the Order. Before long he was granted the rank of Jedi Knight, and following his master's example, he left the Temple for a time, touring the worlds of the Outer Rim to bring peace to turbulent nations. Like Idyth before him, his exploits became known to both Jedi and villain alike; for during this time Sol Mogra shattered a criminal organization that had spanned four systems, bested the Trials of

Herakal, and quashed an uprising on the Sanctic moon of Eremond, amongst many other achievements.

It was only after close to a decade away that Sol Mogra returned to the Temple on Coruscant, where he was received with great warmth. Soon he would take a Padawan of his own and continue to share the legacy of his master with another generation.

However, it was around this time that a dark terror began to plague the lower levels of Coruscant—a cloaked, hooded figure who reveled in violence and lived to excess, and left a tide of bodies in their wake. The people of Coruscant lived in fear, for they knew not when this villain might strike, or what twisted purpose guided their hand. The attacks appeared erratic, each in a different district, with no apparent pattern to the time, place, or choice of victim. The only clue connecting them was that each of the victim's throats had been crushed—that and the reported sightings of the villain, who showed no aversion to being seen in the streets in the vicinity of each attack. It was almost as if the villain was baiting the Jedi, operating openly under their noses.

Thus, Sol Mogra was enlisted to assist in the swift capture of this arrogant terror and to discover more about the villain's origin and the reason behind the attacks, for the Jedi knew that some dark force must be driving such heinous crimes and that only the most trusted amongst them would be able to identify it.

So it was that Sol Mogra went deep into the bowels of the city, down amongst the cutthroats and bounty hunters, the smugglers and crooks. There, he heard talk of a similar figure—a monster of sorts—who had visited those dangerous streets once, many years before, and was reminded of the tales of Master Idyth and how he had tracked and slain a murderous specter before heading off-world in meditative retreat. Stories of the figure had persisted, despite Idyth's victory, and the people were anxious to know what they had done to cause the reappearance of such an evil apparition— for they were convinced the hooded figure and the specter were one and the same.

Sol Mogra returned to the Temple, where he sought the advice of the Masters, but few remembered any facts regarding Idyth's investigation, for he had acted largely alone, and it was so far in the past that the truth had become entwined with the oft-told stories. Idyth had kept no journals, no record of his missions, for in his modesty he had believed that to measure one's life in such a way was to place too much emphasis on the individual when, in truth, a Jedi was nothing more than a sum of all that had come before and all that would come after, a vessel for the Force, with which it might seek balance.

Sol Mogra pondered this during his nightly patrols of the lower levels, fingering the amulet on the cord around his neck and wishing only for the wisdom of his master's counsel. Yet no insight was forthcoming, and the crimes continued. Each night the villain would strike, and each day the reports of sightings would come in, but none of the Jedi patrols could ever track the villain's movements or spy them amongst the ever-shifting crowds.

Never before had Sol Mogra so keenly felt his master's shadow, for he knew the Jedi Council looked to him for a resolution to the nightly terrors, just as they had looked to Master Idyth all those years before. For the first time, Sol Mogra began to wonder whether his association with a renowned hero of the Order was truly such a good thing. For was he not being held in constant comparison with his former master? Was his every action not judged in light of how well he had been taught? He had spent his entire life attempting to live up to Idyth's example—to surpass it, even—but he began to wonder if it was not the ghost of his master who had claimed all the credit.

For it was forever being said of Sol Mogra that his master had taught him well, that he had become a scion of the Order in his master's image. But where was his master now? If Sol Mogra could not find the hooded villain, would he be judged a failure, unworthy of his master's memory?

Such thoughts, he knew, were beneath a Jedi, and he meditated on them, drawing succor from the amulet around his neck, allowing its presence to soothe his mind, to bring him clarity. His master had entrusted him with the treasure, a symbol of his faith that Sol Mogra would prove worthy of it. And had he not? Were his deeds not evidence enough? He had dedicated his life to helping others, to following the Jedi path, to becoming a living embodiment of all that the

Jedi held dear. As Idyth had shown him, Sol Mogra had stared into the darkness and been repulsed by it, had rejected the dark path, shedding all temptation and attachment to any but Idyth himself. He knew in his heart that he was pure, and as he sat in contemplation, cradling the amulet, he allowed all his dark thoughts to bleed away, siphoning off until only peacefulness remained.

Yet Sol Mogra could not shake his deep frustration at his failure to even identify the villain. He wished only to apprehend them, to end their campaign of villainy, and knew that to do it he would need the help of his fellow Jedi. Perhaps, he reasoned, he had taken too much of the burden on himself, focusing on doing as his master had done rather than finding the solution in his own way. Thus, he enlisted the aid of two other Jedi—Kjus Androth and Petano Dreth.

For days, their investigations continued. Nothing else occupied Sol Mogra's mind. And yet the horrors went on and more bodies were discovered. Despite the assistance of the other Jedi, nothing seemed to add up. Sol Mogra knew he was missing something vital, some clue that might set them on the right path to the identity of the villain. He had grown tired, and while at first he dismissed it as naught but weariness and frustration, he could not deny the strange dreams that plagued his sleeping hours.

In them, he walked the streets at night, stalking the hooded figure, always remaining one step behind. The Force was strong with the villain, radiating off them as waves of hate, like a burning aura, infecting the city around them. Sol Mogra would try to keep up, reaching for the villain's shoulder, but always he would be pushed back, fighting ineffectually against whatever dark power held him at bay. He would watch as the villain—whom he now thought to be a man—would select his victim, reaching out a hand, manipulating the Force.

And then he would wake, sweating, crying out— certain that another murder had been committed.

It was after one such dream that Sol Mogra awoke to discover his robes had been torn during the night. There had been no encounter with the villain or any other miscreants during his patrol the previous eve- ning, and he could not recall any incident during which the robes might have been so damaged. Assuming that he had acted in his sleep, perhaps clawing at the robes during the height of his nightmare, he rose and set out to see if there were any new reports of the villain's activity.

It soon became clear that the hooded figure had struck again, and after hurrying to the scene of the crime, he found that the Jedi Kjus Androth had been murdered while on patrol during the night. The hallmark of the shadowy villain was present—the way Kjus's throat had been crushed—but so, too, was a torn fragment of Jedi robes. Petano Dreth had been so distraught that he did not appear to have noticed the dirty rag, abandoned in the gutter, but Sol Mogra recognized it immediately for what it was—a fragment of his own robe. Stunned, his hand went immediately to the amulet around his neck, and he twitched as flickering images from his dream seemed to stutter through his mind, his vision turning momentarily red. He saw the hooded figure bearing down on Kjus in the alleyway, saw his eyes go wide in startled recognition, saw the outstretched hand close into a fist as Kjus clawed at the figure's robes . . . and realized, with dawning terror, that the hand was *his*.

In his mind's eye he saw his cloak swirling around him as he leapt into the pit of a darkened alley; sensed the raw, primal fear of a fleeing victim; heard a shrill scream echo in the night. He pressed his eyes shut, trying to block out the stream of terrifying images, the horror of what he was seeing. Yet still the onslaught came—a vision of glowing yellow eyes in the reflection of a blacked-out window, the sound of panicked footfalls, the adrenaline rush of the pursuit. The visions he'd been seeing in his dreams were not visions at all but twisted memories replaying his own horrifying actions as he chased down his victims in the streets. He wanted to scream, to deny it all, but he knew it was the truth. He had been the villain all along.

Appalled, Sol Mogra staggered back, releasing his grip on the amulet. Immediately, the darkness fell away, his mind clearing, and he knew then that the relic, with its glittering eye of kyber, was to blame for the terrifying fracturing of his soul.

This, then, had been his master's secret all

along—that the amulet had become a repository for all Idyth's anger and fear and that, instead of facing such things as a Jedi must, Idyth had buried them deep in the relic, presenting only his virtuous self to the universe. While he was lauded as a paragon of the Order, all those dark emotions simmered and grew darker still until they had attained such pressure that they sought release. Thus, by day Idyth had served as the selfless Jedi he had always been known as, but by night he had become a thing of darkness, stalking the lower levels of the city. This had been the specter Idyth had supposedly defeated before taking himself off to another world, where no further questions might be asked.

In taking on his master's role and adopting both

the amulet and Idyth's ways—for had Sol Mogra not looked often into that dark mirror, pushing away his darkest impulses?—the Padawan had truly followed in his master's footsteps, attaining glory and recognition by day and becoming subsumed by his darkest emotions at night.

In making that bleak and startling discovery, in recognizing the true horror of both his and his master's failure and the terrible acts they had committed, Sol Mogra knew he could never face his Jedi masters, for the shame had already begun to consume him and would burn him up from inside, twisting him into a thing of hate. Instead, he clutched the amulet, holding it close to his heart, allowing the darkness within it to flow out and dominate him forever. He fled into the night, giving in to all his most terrible fears and his rage.

It is whispered that he is still out there, somewhere, a creature of the shadows, forever clutching the amulet that sealed his doom and driven only by his instincts toward the dark side.

THE GILDED CAGE

HERE WAS ONCE A
Sith Lord by the name of Darth
Caldoth, whose activities had,
during his long and event-
ful career, given rise to a great number of enemies.
Throughout the galactic core, there were many
who had just cause to abhor Caldoth and his malign
schemes—from Jedi Knights to Serulean assassins,
from Muldorean crime lords to the Seven Kings of
Illmuth. Of all these worthy enemies, however, none
were more cunning and vengeful than the Nightsisters
of Dathomir.

The Nightsisters had long before adopted a practice of mummifying their dead and committing them to pods of animal skin, which they hung from structures that resembled trees, decorated with tassels and animal bones. In times of extreme crisis, these dead Nightsisters could be resurrected, stirring from their pods like nightmarish shadowmoths to defend their living sisters.

When Darth Caldoth, intent on learning the secrets of the Nightsisters' reanimation process, made a daring incursion into their graveyard on Dathomir and stole away with a pod containing the mummified remains of a fallen sister, the witches viewed it as an act of war.

Yet the Nightsisters were patient and knew that the

time would eventually come for them to make good their revenge. So it was that they plotted and waited until they believed Darth Caldoth to be at his most vulnerable, having recently suffered a terrible defeat at the hands of the Jedi.

Caldoth had become aware of a rare fragment of fresco relating to the ancients and their use of the Force that had been uncovered during a Jedi expedition and transferred to their temple on Bathoris. So it was that Caldoth launched an attack on the temple, intent on causing enough of a distraction that he might steal away with the artifact in the chaos.

The surprise attack went well—for the Jedi had never anticipated such a bold move—and Caldoth had come close to securing his objective. Swathes of

Temple Guards had fallen, along with several Jedi Knights, but there was one amongst the Jedi, by the name of Bran Ath' Morath, who had held his ground, repelling Caldoth from the inner sanctum and locking him in a desperate duel until enough of the remaining Jedi could rally and Caldoth was forced to retreat or else face capture.

As a result, Caldoth was shaken, both from his defeat at the hands of Bran Ath' Morath and his singular failure to retrieve the object he so desired.

Seeing this—for they had kept an almost constant eye on Caldoth during the intervening time—the Nightsisters enacted the first stage of their revenge.

A gathering was called, during which six chosen sisters were subjected to a series of trials that would test their mental and physical fortitude. After a night of great hardship, bound to stone pillars and assailed by the spirits of their dead sisters, forced to suffer horrific hallucinations and relive the memories of those they had vanquished, one sister emerged victorious. This sister, Zeldin, was cut down from her pillar and taken away to be prepared for all that would follow.

Zeldin was still young, having barely attained adulthood, yet she was strong and had long been marked for greatness by the elders of the coven. Nevertheless, she slept fitfully that day as she recovered from her trials, plagued by dreams of torment—not at the hands of the ghosts that had assailed her but by her fated enemy, Darth Caldoth, whom she feared above all else. Yet she knew there could be no turning back, for the vengeance of the Nightsisters was absolute and failure would lead to terrors of a different kind.

The very next night the coven gathered once again, only this time to add their voices in support of Zeldin as she enacted a ritual to place herself in a deep trance, translating her thoughts into the Living Force. Her task was to inveigle her way into the mind of Darth Caldoth, to breach his mental barriers so she might influence him from afar, coercing the Sith Lord into doing the Nightsisters' bidding. Ultimately, their aim was simple: to ruin Darth Caldoth from within and, over time, drive him toward his own destruction.

The Nightsisters were well aware of Darth Caldoth's formidable power and had plotted accordingly. Zeldin's influence—once she had eased the tendrils of her thoughts into Caldoth's mind—was to be only the lightest of touches. She would make no move that he might detect, for to give herself away would lead to ruin, both for the plan and for the coven. To incur Darth Caldoth's wrath would be to rain devastation on Dathomir.

Carefully, then, empowered by the support of her coven yet filled with trepidation, Zeldin extended her thoughts. To the delight of her sisters the first tentative fingers of influence proved more than successful and Darth Caldoth easier than anticipated to steer.

For some time Zeldin continued in this way, nudging the occasional decision in a different direction and subtly altering the course of Darth Caldoth's life. As time went on Zeldin's influence grew, as did her confidence, for even as she became more active in her interference, it appeared to pass unnoticed by Caldoth, whose attentions remained distant. Soon the time came for a more concerted step.

Thus, the coven gathered to enact a ritual of prognostication, reaching out into the Force to seek a furtive glimpse into the future, to identify the alternate paths along which they could encourage Darth Caldoth, leading him ever closer to ruination. In such a way the Nightsisters identified a young Twi'lek named Ry Nymbis, who might appear to Caldoth as the perfect candidate for a new apprentice but who the Nightsisters divined would eventually turn on his master and seek to claim Caldoth's power as his own.

So it was that Zeldin set to work infiltrating

Caldoth's thoughts, insinuating and suggesting, leading him most gently into the orbit of the youth. Satisfied with their work, the Nightsisters watched from afar as the apprentice was schooled in the dark side, learning to harness his rage and fear as he assisted Caldoth in the quest to recover ever more knowledge of the ancient arts.

Yet as Ry Nymbis grew, so did his ambition until such a point that—as the Nightsisters had anticipated—the Twi'lek began to covet the power of his master. Thus, much to Zeldin's delight, Ry Nymbis stole a ritual from his master's books, lured Caldoth to a lonely outcropping, and enacted the ancient spell.

The ritual misfired, however, reflecting back on

its caster and turning Ry Nymbis to stone. Caldoth, amused by his apprentice's miscalculation, left the calcified figure where it stood as a warning to all those who might attempt to cross him in the future.

The Nightsisters raged, for their patience had borne no fruit. Yet still they were not to be dissuaded from their plan, for their memories were long and their hunger for vengeance even longer. Thus, another ritual of prognostication was enacted, and this time in the vapors the elders of the coven glimpsed the possibility of another trap, which Zeldin was soon tasked to lay.

Caldoth's hunger for the knowledge of the ancients was well-known—for he sought in such knowledge the means of achieving long-forgotten mastery over others—and he had dedicated many years of his life to searching for the relics left behind by those races that had long before breathed their last in the galaxy. Such finds were exceedingly rare and often dangerous to acquire, protected by curses, traps, or guardians, and the Nightsisters had become aware of one such relic—a totem dating back many thousands of generations—which they knew lay amongst the shattered remnants of a temple on the storm-racked moon of Obsidia. More than that, though, they had seen in their vision that the relic was protected by the guardian spirit of one of the ancient monks who had once attended the temple, and so powerful was this spirit in the Force that if Caldoth visited the moon he risked obliteration at its hands.

Once again, Zeldin carefully extended her influence, leading Caldoth on a journey of discovery—for the Nightsisters' plan would only work if Caldoth truly believed he had uncovered the existence of the relic through his own divination and research. Much time passed as she guided him on this course, stirring his passion for the quest, encouraging him down particular routes in his research, until at last the breakthrough occurred and Caldoth found an ancient tablet that pointed to the existence of the relic. Overjoyed, he at once made plans to travel to Obsidia to retrieve it. Yet his research had made no mention of the guardian spirit the Nightsisters had witnessed in their vision, so Zeldin encouraged him on, hopeful that Caldoth was finally about to walk into her trap.

So it was that Caldoth made the arduous journey to the wastes of Wild Space, taking his shuttle deep into the Unknown Regions, through the Straits of Hibrath and beyond, until at last Obsidia appeared before him.

The small moon orbited a tempestuous gas giant that in turn circled a weak sun, bloated and dying from the extremes of age. The gravitational pressures were slowly tearing the gas giant asunder, and the resulting storms caused the moon—formed of a glistening black rock—to judder constantly, its orbit slowly decaying as it tumbled ponderously toward its mother planet.

There was the resting place of the totem the Nightsisters had seen during their ritual, and it was there Zeldin had led Caldoth to die in his attempt to retrieve it.

Demonstrating great skill in his piloting, Caldoth took his shuttle down to the moon's surface and landed it amongst the sprawling temple ruins—for his research had been thorough and he knew for what and where he looked. Zeldin was all too aware of the risks of allowing Caldoth to obtain such a powerful relic, yet she knew also that as soon as Caldoth attempted to claim it, the guardian spirit would show itself and strike down the unwary Sith Lord.

Sure enough, the totem was housed in a decorated alcove inside the shell of the ruined temple, in which plant life had run wild, pushing up the flagstones to overrun the entire structure. Caldoth passed unhin-dered, causing the vines and boughs to part in his wake as he approached the totem, his eyes shining at the sight of it.

It was then that Zeldin sensed something was wrong. Caldoth, upon reaching the alcove, twisted on the spot, drawing a large vial from his robes and chanting the words of an arcane binding ritual in the ancient language of the Nightsisters—a ritual that should have been unknown to all but the Dathomirian witches themselves.

The guardian spirit—a huge phantasmagorical entity formed of swirling mists, with a gnashing crocodilian face—had seeped through the temple's ceiling to manifest behind Caldoth, reaching out for him just as it appeared that Caldoth had been about to snatch up the totem. Caught off guard, however, and entrapped by the binding words in Caldoth's ritual, the entity wailed as it was drawn into the vial in the Sith Lord's hands, its vapors swirling behind the glass walls of its new prison. Smiling, Caldoth stoppered the vial and slipped it back inside his robes. He returned to his shuttle with his prize, leaving the ancient totem sitting in its alcove, undisturbed.

Zeldin raged in frustration, for once again Darth Caldoth had overturned her expectations, seeking not the relic but the guardian spirit itself, which he might interrogate for clues to its original form and bind to do his bidding. In this he had made use of the Nightsisters' own rituals, although it remained unclear to Zeldin exactly how the Sith had acquired that knowledge.

The Nightsisters' impatience grew thin, for their nemesis continued to grow in strength and power despite their continued interference. A final ritual was performed to grant further insight into Caldoth's possible fate, and to their glee, the Nightsisters' were granted a vision of Caldoth being run through with a lightsaber. The weapon belonged to none other than the Jedi Knight Bran Ath' Morath, who had been one of the few to defeat Caldoth during the time of the Nightsisters' observations.

It was decided, then, that Zeldin would seek to steer Caldoth toward one final trap. If the Nightsisters could lead the Jedi to unwittingly enact their revenge for them, then all the better. All that remained was for Zeldin to inspire in Caldoth a desire to destroy the Jedi who had beaten him at the temple on Bathoris all those years before.

This proved a simple task, for Zeldin knew all there was to know about revenge. She infiltrated Caldoth's dreams, stoking the fires of hatred, planting the seeds of a vendetta that took no time at all to bloom.

Before long, Caldoth had concocted his plan. He would lure Bran Ath' Morath away from Bathoris through a campaign of activity on the neighboring world of Kizan. If he revealed his own hand in the proceedings, then surely Bran Ath' Morath would come to seek him out, to finish what they had begun all those years before.

So it was that Caldoth made haste for Kizan, where the glass towers of the cities scratched the undersides of the very clouds and all was peaceful, for it was a place of knowledge, where students traveled from all across the galaxy to learn the philosophies of different cultures. There Caldoth set about his campaign to lure the Jedi, and within hours of his arrival, Pundith, the central city on the subtropical peninsula, had been reduced to nothing but glass shards and debris. Yet Caldoth had been careful to be seen during this terrible assault, knowing well that word would soon reach the Jedi temple on Bathoris, and knowing who would be the nearest and most ready to respond.

Sure enough, the Jedi ships soon appeared in orbit, and Caldoth—who had remained amongst the ruins of Pundith to await them—grinned, knowing that the hour of his revenge was upon him. Secretly, Zeldin allowed herself a smile, too, confident that Caldoth's death was a certainty, for had the Nightsisters not seen Bran Ath' Morath run the Sith Lord through with his lightsaber?

Four of the Jedi deployed, and three were dealt with in short order by Caldoth's red blade, for they were no match for his skills or for the power of his anger and the burning blasts of ferocious energy that would burst from his fingertips. Yet one proved less easy to snare, for Bran Ath' Morath had indeed come to Kizan to face his old foe, and his abilities were more than a match for those of the Sith Lord. Caldoth seethed with a hatred stoked by the intruder in his mind yet fueled by the power of the dark side. As the two masters clashed amongst the glittering ruins they fell into the thrust and parry of an elaborate dance, wheeling and striking with their lightsabers in a momentous battle that saw the landscape around them ripple with the outpouring of their power. So evenly matched were they that their duel raged on and on, sending them diving and soaring amongst the despoiled rooftops, clashing in the narrow alleyways, weaving in and out of the shattered remnants of buildings.

As the light began to fade and the day gave way to dusk, Zeldin knew that the killing blow was close, for both Sith and Jedi had begun to tire. She, too, had grown weary, as if the simple act of witnessing the battle had sapped her strength and fortitude—as if, in some strange way, her own well of hatred and fear was somehow replenishing Caldoth.

Yet Zeldin could not have anticipated how deep Caldoth's anger ran or how assured he was of his own superiority, for seeing there would be no end to the battle unless he was able to surprise his opponent, Caldoth lowered his blade and thrust himself forward, piercing himself through the shoulder with Bran Ath' Morath's yellow blade.

The Jedi looked down in shock to see his lightsaber jutting from Caldoth's back, but it was the last thing he saw, for Caldoth had anticipated the Jedi's shocked response at his supposed victory and removed Bran Ath' Morath's head with a sweep of his red blade before falling back, wounded but nevertheless alive.

On Dathomir, Zeldin screamed in frustration, and

the Nightsisters flocked around her, offering comfort, for they knew what must be done and how much it would tax their sister's abilities to do it.

Following the battle on Kizan, Zeldin and her sisters prepared. For what felt to her an age, a small part of herself had existed with Darth Caldoth's mind, the lightest of presences, observing, nudging, and influencing. But the patience of the Nightsisters was exhausted, and the time had come for more drastic measures. She would attempt to increase her presence in Caldoth's mind and assert full control over both his mind and body through the act of possession. She would make him a prisoner of the Nightsisters and effect his complete and utter ruin.

So the ritual began, and the whole coven gathered

in the caves to lend their strength to Zeldin. She reached out with her mind, at first gently, then more fully, probing deep into the crevices of Caldoth's thoughts as he rested in his floating laboratory complex on Athamar.

Darth Caldoth's mind, however, was well-tempered and strong, and Zeldin was forced to push harder and harder to meet her ends, until such a point that she had almost entirely given up possession of her own physical form to better influence his. He fought back, engaging her in a duel of the senses, attempting to push her away, but Zeldin had come to know Caldoth well, and she understood his weaknesses better even than she understood her own. Slowly she pushed for dominance, and to her relief, Caldoth began to give way as his mental barriers crumbled. She rejoiced as his mind finally buckled and bent to her will and she found herself in full possession of his body and mind.

Yet Zeldin's triumph was short-lived, for even as she seized control, she sensed that all was not as it seemed. Inwardly, Caldoth drew a wicked smile, and Zeldin recoiled.

It was then that he acted, for in truth Darth Caldoth had been mindful of Zeldin's presence all along, ever since her first tentative engagements all those years before. He had drawn on her strength and knowledge, first making use of the binding ritual buried deep in her consciousness to trap the spirit on Obsidia and then calling on her reserves to fuel his own battle with the Jedi. Indeed, he had manipulated her, allowing her to grow increasingly confident and push deeper into his mind until the point where she became vulnerable. For Darth Caldoth's mastery of the Force was far superior to that of the Nightsisters, and with it, he drew a gilded cage around Zeldin's disembodied presence in his mind, trapping her there, separated from her body and unable to influence the actions of her terrible host.

Zeldin screamed, panicked and afraid, trying desperately to withdraw, to pull her consciousness back into her own body on Dathomir. But the bonds had been severed, and there was to be no escape. Terrified, Zeldin raged, but Caldoth's grip on her was absolute, and no longer could she assert any influence over his thoughts or his physical form. She was trapped in a prison of her own devising, and there was no hope that she would ever be free again. All she could do was scream.

From that day forth, Zeldin was forced to exist in the permanent prison of the Sith Lord's mind, cut off from her sisters and the outside world. Zeldin's sisters did not come to her aid, so terrified were they of Darth Caldoth's dreadful power. Her body was committed to a pod and hung on the very same structure from which Caldoth had first stolen the mummified remains of Zeldin's sister. She was never heard from again—except by Darth Caldoth, who from time to time was given to listen to her screams and smile.

A LIFE IMMORTAL

ONG AGO, WHEN THE galaxy was young and the stars burned bright and new, there lived a Sith Lord by the name of Darth Noctyss.

Celebrated and abhorred in equal measure—for even as a young woman her power set her apart from others—Darth Noctyss had long carved a path of red destruction through the Inner Rim. Worlds fell to her sickle-bladed lightsaber, and the ruins of the civilization of Ivis stand as testament to her hatred.

Noctyss's capacity for channeling the dark side of

the Force seemed almost limitless, and all who stood in her way soon wilted . . . if they remained in possession of their heads. It was said that, in those early days, Darth Noctyss might have conquered the entire galaxy, forging a brutal realm of the Sith that would have dominated for eons—if only she had had a mind to do it.

Yet, although Noctyss knew the temptations of power all too well—like any who give themselves to the dark side, she was not immune to its call—she desired one thing above all others: the perpetuation of her own life.

What use, she claimed, was a kingdom if one day she would no longer remain to shape it? What use all that power if it might not stave off the inevitable, encroaching degradations of age? Empires could wait—for when she achieved her true purpose, immortality, then would she have all the time she wished to conquer and reforge the galaxy in her image.

Thus, Noctyss passed her days in pursuit of her singular goal, obsessively seeking out the relics of ages gone by, the fragmentary records of ancient races that once knew the secrets of the Force but were now lost to the turning of the spheres and the long seasons of the universe. She refused to take on an apprentice, preferring to study in solitude, absorbing all that she could of the long-forgotten rituals that might lead her closer to her chosen goal.

Years passed in this way, until Noctyss herself had reached the autumn of her life, having used what dark arts she had uncovered to extend her physical form beyond its natural span. She knew, however, that she was close to the answers she had sought for so long— for her research on the desert planet Jaguada had shown her the way to a place named Exegol, a distant world steeped in the rich history of the Sith and imbued with their diabolical, mystical power.

So it was that Noctyss set out, alone, for Exegol. There, she knew, she would complete her work and uncover the final pieces of the ritual that would see her live forever.

Exegol is a blighted place, its atmosphere charged with fierce electrical storms, its surface ravaged by the excavations carried out there by the Sith. Deep inside the heart of the planet, however, Noctyss found evidence of a crumbling citadel filled with towering statuary and long deserted—or so she thought.

For months Noctyss explored these ruins, the only signs of life the rat-grubs that scrabbled amongst the cracks and crevices, and the faint whispering that filled her head whenever she attempted to sleep—the gnawing of a thousand other minds, chattering at the edges of her consciousness. There on Exegol, the veil between life and death was thin, and Noctyss knew that she drew closer to success with every passing day and every cavern she explored.

Sure enough, during one such expedition amongst the flooded halls of the lower chambers, Noctyss found what she had been searching for—although at the time she did not know it.

It began with a splash of movement in the gloaming—the sound of a foot stirring the puddles of floodwater that had settled between the broken flagstones. Noctyss, who had failed to sense the thing's presence, spun, igniting the blade of her lightsaber and baring her teeth, ready to join in battle with the newcomer.

Yet the wretched thing exposed by the crimson light of her blade presented no threat, for it was a broken, stooped creature—the remnants of what had perhaps once been a man but was now little more than a feral beast. Its spine was twisted at an unusual angle, causing it to hunch forward so that its left shoulder dipped almost to its knees. Its flesh was pallid and translucent, shriveled and wrinkled so that its immense age was evident, but unreadable. Its stringy hair fell in strands down the side of its face, limp and thick with grime. It wore only rags that might once have been fashioned as clothes. It staggered toward her, clawed fingers outstretched, and Noctyss raised her lightsaber, ready to strike the thing down, to put it out of its misery. Something stilled her hand, however—some deep sense that the creature might yet have a bearing on her quest—and as it whimpered inanely, shambling along the passageway in the gloom, she lowered her blade and beckoned it forward. It stopped before her, regarding her with rheumy eyes, and mumbled a word that, to Noctyss's ears, sounded something akin to *mistress*.

At this, a sly smile spread across Noctyss's face, for she saw immediately that the pitiable creature might be put to use as a servant or slave—to aid her in her quest.

Sure enough, the creature soon proved its worth; as if it somehow knew instinctively what Noctyss sought, it turned and led her along the darkened corridors beneath the citadel, deeper and deeper into that strange realm, through the thickening darkness and cold, past the last of the lapping floodwater, and into a small system of meticulously carved chambers.

The tunnels were labyrinthine and disorienting, and as Noctyss followed, she heard the whispering once more—only this time the voices were like a tight pressure building inside her skull, growing ever more anxious, urging her on, deeper and farther. And yet, somehow, these voices were a comfort, too—an echo of those who had trodden this pathway before her, and who, even now, were urging her on toward greatness.

At last, the shambling creature drew to a halt, swaying steadily on the spot, a wretched grin writ large on its malformed lips. Noctyss stopped, taking a moment to examine her surroundings. She had long since lost any sense of how deep below the planet's surface they stood or, indeed, how far they had ventured from the relative simplicity of the main citadel—but there, down amongst the bowels of the planet, she found herself in a laboratory of sorts. The walls were emblazoned with the oldest of Sith runes, and the floor—covered in a thick layer of dust and detritus—had once been marked out in a symbolic set of interlocking circles. Bottles and jars filled with unidentifiable tinctures cluttered obsidian work surfaces, and crumbling tomes, bound in cracked hide of some kind and covered in a thick smear of spiderwebs, sat on a crooked wooden shelf. Something that had once been flesh and blood but had long before putrefied, sat suspended in a filthy tank of some substance unknown.

How had the creature known about this place? And who had left it in such a way?

Noctyss approached one of the surfaces, running her fingertips lightly over the fragile pages that had spilled from one of the disintegrating books. There, she immediately recognized the designs she had long before committed to memory—designs she had first seen on Malachor and that had set her on the first steps of the journey that had ended on Exegol.

Someone had been there before her, pursuing the same ends. They had led the way! This, then, was their abandoned laboratory—the place where they had finally solved the riddles of the past, where they had broken the chains that tethered them to mortal life and set themselves free. There, amongst that glorious mess, were the answers she had sought for so long.

The creature emitted a wet giggle, and Noctyss laughed, for what else could the thing be but the servant of the Sith who had once inhabited this place? A being dragged from the pit of filth where it had been born, brought there to serve. It was nothing but a wretch, the very dregs of life, a thing so broken that it barely clung to its existence—and now it was hers, to do with as she pleased. She would start by having it clean the laboratory while she set about examining the old texts for any clue to what the previous inhabitant had been doing.

Thus, much time passed, and as Noctyss buried herself in her research, the creature scampered around her, scrubbing floors, lugging loads, and otherwise carrying out all the miserable tasks that might keep Noctyss from her work.

She grew thin, forgoing all sustenance other than knowledge, for she knew that she was closer than she had ever been, and while the passage of time locked in that lightless chamber proved unkind—her back growing stiff, her muscles soft—she did not give it even a passing thought. She berated the creature almost daily, taking out her frustrations on the abominable thing, but so starved was it for attention that it would kneel feebly before her, head bowed, a strange, ineffable smile on its face.

This creature, this mutant, had nothing to offer the galaxy, no reason to exist beyond its servitude to her. This, she decided, was how she would rule, once the ritual was complete—she would take her place at the head of a vast realm of the Sith, and all her many subjects would be shown their place, would kneel before her in gratitude for their enlightenment. It would be an unending kingdom, for she would sit on her throne unchallenged and undying—the very heart of the galaxy over which she would rule. That was true power, the only power she had ever sought: the power over life and death itself.

And so it went on, as, slowly, Noctyss pieced together the final elements of the puzzle, understanding at long last the ritual she must complete to transcend. The work carried out by her forebear, Darth Sanguis, whose records she had found there on Exegol, had provided the final elements she required.

His research had been most thorough, and she would trail the steps he had taken before her. She would follow his path toward greatness.

The incantations would take three days. After that, all she needed was a worthy tribute, a willing sacrifice to offer up their life force and complete the rite. There on Exegol such life was sparse, but fortune had granted her a final boon, and the skulking creature she had found in the tunnels would serve its mistress one last time. At the culmination of the rite, she would absorb its essence and use it to remold her very soul. This was her right, her purpose. This was everything she had given her entire life for.

So it was that the preparations began, and the creature, ignorant of its coming fate, slaved long and hard to anticipate Noctyss's every need. As she spoke the ancient, rasping words of the incantation, she felt the voices in her head join with her, until the chant became a cacophony—a choir of voices, dragging her toward the precipice of eternal life. Indeed, the words seemed to take on a life of their own, and soon Noctyss could no longer tell if she was leading the chorus of voices or if they were leading her. Yet the ripples of energy that pulsed beneath her skin were exultant, enough to drive any and all doubt from her mind. Time lost all form. There were no minutes, hours, or days—there were simply the ritual and the words and the power.

And then the moment was upon her. Noctyss opened her eyes, breathing steadily as she sought the creature—only to find it had anticipated even this final need. It rested before her on its knees, its crooked back drawn straight, its fingers pulling at the fabric of its rotten clothes to expose the milky-white flesh of its chest—and still that strange smile on its lips.

Noctyss gave a final sigh of satisfaction and then drew her dagger and plunged it deep into the creature's heart.

For a moment, nothing happened. Then the entire chamber seemed to erupt in sparking energy that burst forth from the creature's chest, coursing up Noctyss's arm, flowing over her body, seeping into her flesh. She felt invigorated, alive in a way she had never felt before, and she laughed, relishing the sensation of her burgeoning life force.

She felt her body begin to shift and change, remodeling itself as the vital energy flowed into her, rejuvenating her tired form, rendering her fresh and new again. Inside her head, the voices cried out in triumph, cheering in ecstasy at her success. Everything she had foretold would come to pass. Soon she would rise to become the master of all things.

But then the cries of joy became cries of anguish, and Noctyss screamed as she felt her body jerk and spasm. Something was wrong.

The voices were screaming, pitiful and full of remorse. Dawning horror filled Noctyss's thoughts. Had she mispronounced a vital phrase during the preparations? Was the creature's life force not enough?

She felt her spine shift, twisting, rotating—and she bellowed in agony. She tried to focus, tried to fight the rising tide of panic, to push away the energy coursing through her, to stop the ritual . . . but it was too late. Her flesh crawled, pulling back painfully against her bones, shriveling and wrinkling. She held her hands up before her, still swirling in the crackling energy, only to watch as they contorted, becoming spindly, talon-like things. The breath seemed to rush out of her lungs as her ribs contracted, and it felt for a moment as if the blood in her veins were boiling her alive from the inside. She screamed again, calling out for help until her throat was raw, but there was no one there to hear her.

As the energy fizzed and crackled to a stop, Noctyss felt blackness envelop her, pulling her heavily toward the ground.

Sometime later, Noctyss woke to the sound of scratching. Startled, she raised her head, wincing at the lancing pain the movement sent through her neck. The rat-grubs had gathered and were crawling on the body of the creature before her on the floor. She scrabbled up, shuffling back, her movements jarring and painful. She tried to mumble something, but her words were malformed and issued only as a slur.

Horrified, she reached for the edge of the obsidian workbench, pulling herself awkwardly to her feet. The back of her neck prickled with fear; terror gripped her heart. What had happened? What had become of her? Had the ritual worked?

She swept her arm across the surface, searching hurriedly for a looking glass. She grasped it in her spidery fingers and, fearful of what she might find, held it up in the thin light of the chamber, peering warily at her own reflection.

With a mournful wail, Noctyss cast the looking glass against the wall, watching the splinters shower to the floor. She turned to look at the body of the creature, at the wicked grin still there on its twisted face.

It had known all along. It had understood the path she walked, and it had encouraged her at each step, as a means to seek its own freedom. For now she, too, understood the truth—that this was no creature, but what was left of her predecessor, Darth Sanguis—the Sith Lord who, like Noctyss, had wanted to live forever. And follow in his footsteps she had, for now she, too, was like him—a twisted, grotesque version of her former self, cursed to eke out a painful, lonely existence in the bowels of Exegol.

Noctyss had given her entire life in pursuit of the secret of immortality, ignoring all else, sundering entire worlds in her quest to live forever. And now the voices whispered that she had earned what she had so long desired: she was as close to immortality as one could be, destined to live a life undying and yet unable to truly live.

ABOUT THE AUTHOR

GEORGE MANN is a *Sunday Times* bestselling novelist and scriptwriter, and he's loved *Star Wars* for about as long as he's been able to walk. He wishes he still had the Ewok village action figure set he adored when he was a boy.

He previously teamed up with Grant Griffin for *Star Wars: Myths & Fables*, and is the author of the Newbury & Hobbes Victorian mystery series, as well as four novels about a 1920s vigilante known as the Ghost. He's also written best-selling *Doctor Who* novels, new adventures for Sherlock Holmes, and the supernatural mystery series Wychwood.

His comic writing includes extensive work on *Doctor Who*, *Dark Souls*, *Warhammer 40,000*, and *Newbury & Hobbes*, as well as *Teenage Mutant Ninja Turtles* and *Star Wars Adventures* for younger readers.

He's written audio scripts for *Doctor Who*, *Blake's 7*, *Sherlock Holmes*, *Warhammer 40,000*, and more.

As editor, he's assembled four anthologies of original Sherlock Holmes fiction, as well as multiple volumes of *The Solaris Book of New Science Fiction* and *The Solaris Book of New Fantasy*.

You can find him on Twitter @George_Mann.

ABOUT THE ILLUSTRATOR

GRANT GRIFFIN is a freelance illustrator living in Nicaragua. He has been carving out a niche in the fantasy and science fiction genre since 2013, which spans both games and publishing. Along with his first feature with Disney • Lucasfilm Press, illustrating *Star Wars: Myths and Fables*, his work has been featured on covers of titles published by Becker&Mayer, Black Library, Green Ronin Publishing, and Centipede Press.